For Sarah

Some   ow

C000077198

Hope

Trudie x

TAKE MY HAND

...and other short stories

by

Trudie Ellen Thomas

Illustrated by

Jordan Thomas

POLARITY

PUBLISHING

Orders: Please contact Polarity Publishing via the email address:
Orders@polaritypublishing.co.uk

ISBN: 978-1-9995810-6-0

First published 2022

Copyright © 2022 Trudie Ellen Thomas. All rights reserved.

All rights reserved. Apart from any permitted use under UK
copyright law, no part of this publication may be reproduced or
transmitted in any form or by any means, electronic or mechanical,
including photocopying, recording, or any information, storage or
retrieval system, without permission in writing from the publisher
or under licence from the Copyright Licensing Agency Limited.
Further details of such licenses (for reprographic reproduction)
may be obtained from the Copyright Licensing Agency Ltd, Saffron
House, 6-10 Kirby Street, London EC1N 8TS.

For Roger, my dad.
Where my love of stories began.

Trudie is a Welsh gal, who now lives in Buckinghamshire with her family and their Tibetan Terrier Winifred. She writes in her shed at the bottom of her garden - in true Roald Dahl style.

She loves writing fiction, short stories and both children's and adult novels. She also writes a regular feature for her village magazine - entitled Trudie Talks To... about local residents who have special talents or gifts.

Previously, an English teacher she now works as an Extra (Supporting Artist) providing her with plenty of time to read and write in between takes. Her favourite role being a Muggle on Platform 9 3/4. She has lots of lovely writing buddies and constantly feels wrapped in a hug from their encouraging words of wisdom.

Trudie can often be found in a cozy cafe, getting comfy with a frothy cappuccino, a warm chocolate brownie and a great new book on de-cluttering. Sadly, her home remains quite messy!

Get in touch with Trudie at trudieethomas@aol.com She would love to hear which of her twelve short stories is your favourite!

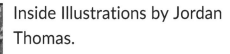 Inside Illustrations by Jordan Thomas.

I couldn't be happier to collaborate with my mum and help bring her stories to life. I've had so much fun illustrating these and even more fun reading them.

Like my work? Drop me a message on LinkedIn https://www.linkedin.com/in/dzynestudios

CONTENTS

THE TUESDAY WALKERS

'**D**amn and blast it,' Hazel cursed, as her front gate swung shut behind her, but her body lurched sideways. Hazel crumpled to the ground. And if it wasn't bad enough that one of her carrier bags had split open, and her costly braeburns were rolling down the garden path, she could now hear Audrey coming.

She must have been curtain-twitching again and seen her fall, Hazel thought as she tried to scramble to her feet – but failed.

Audrey, Hazel's next-door-neighbour of too many years, had the persistence of a hungry bird spying a wriggling worm. And right now, Hazel was that very worm without an escape hole in sight.

Hazel made a grab for the box of chocolate fingers, and in a moment of sheer panic shoved it under her jumper. Then, just as Audrey managed to negotiate Hazel's sticky gate-latch in one easy movement, Hazel spotted her trio of walnut whips. She managed to push them up the sleeve of her coat just in time.

'Oh, poor you,' Audrey fussed, placing a handkerchief on the path, before kneeling at Hazel's side. 'Took another tumble, did we?'

'Well not exactly.' Hazel flushed pink. 'My brolly caught in my bag as I tried to get through that useless gate, then my hip did that clicky thing, it does from time to time and sent me to the ground again.'

Having sailed through it without a problem, Audrey glanced back at the gate and frowned. Although with her tightly pinned-back hair her forehead hardly moved, leaving her eyebrows to do all the work.

'If you say so,' Audrey said, sounding as if she had an entirely different theory of how Hazel had ended up sitting on a garden path on a cold, and wet, February afternoon. Her excess weight was Hazel's best guess. She would never forget Audrey's whispered observation at George's graveside, that if Hazel had worn a slightly larger coat, she would have been able to do up *all* the buttons. That bit of neighbourly advice had made Hazel so angry she had nearly pushed Audrey in after George. 'Now, how about I help you inside?' Audrey said, tucking her hands under Hazel's armpits.

Hazel suppressed a groan; the last thing she needed now was her salad-loving neighbour poking her nose into her kitchen cupboards, and passing judgement on the contents of her fridge. Let alone all the yummy goodies Hazel had just purchased.

'That's really not necessary,' Hazel tried, hugging the one bag that hadn't split to her chest to hopefully conceal its contents. It felt cold. No wonder, she thought picturing the large bag of frozen chips and the strawberry pavlova inside.

'It's no trouble,' Audrey insisted. 'We'll get you inside and you can take the weight off your feet whilst I unpack your groceries.'

Hazel sighed; there was no point arguing with Audrey – she always won.

'Alright,' Hazel agreed, but cringing again as she spotted another stray item. A carton of milk which had managed to crash-land near George's prize chrysanthemums. Although sadly these days, under Hazel's non-watchful care, she doubted would make it through the turnstile of the village fete, let alone win best-in-show.

'Can you just rescue my milk, please?' Hazel pointed to the carton lying upside down in the dirt.

She watched Audrey use her long skinny finger to hook it out from its resting place, her eyebrows hitching as she read the label: Full Fat Vanilla Milkshake. *Oh no.*

Three hours later and Hazel collapsed onto her sofa, exhausted. Audrey had finally gone. Although, getting her to leave had come at a price. After listening to an endless list of benefits, Hazel eventually said yes to joining Audrey's walking group: the Tuesday Walkers.

Eleven able-bodied, and *super friendly* folk, Audrey had enthused. The addition of Hazel would make her TW's, as she affectionately called them, the perfect dozen.

Perhaps a weekly hike might be just the thing to help her shed a pound or two, Hazel considered, whilst eyeing a baking-tray sat on top of the oven. Cooling down nicely and loaded with Hazel's homemade butter-shortbread, all ready to dip into her coco before bed.

Alright, alright, Audrey, she told her neighbour, yes, *I'll join!*

After the first walk, an hour and a half of wellie-rubbing torture, Hazel was ready to quit. But Audrey was having none of it, and having presented herself on Hazel's doorstep, a record-breaking twenty-one times that week – Hazel promised to give the walking group one more try.

So, the following Tuesday, Hazel arrived at the TW's designated starting point, Buckthorn Woods car park again, determined to do her very best to enjoy herself this time. Hazel was perched on the edge of her open car-boot, tightening her shoelaces in readiness for walk number two, when Oliver, the only man in the group strolled over.

'Ah, trainers,' he said, pointing to Hazel's feet as if she might need help locating them, 'an interesting choice.'

'Thanks,' she said, pleasantly surprised that someone had made the effort to talk to her. Along with the painful mistake of wearing Wellington boots on her first walk, Hazel had been disappointed that Audrey's promise to meet *super friendly folk*, had not transpired. Even when Hazel had offered them a choice of snacks on route, they seemed more interested in fungi and wood-pigeon feathers.

Audrey gave two sharp short bursts on her whistle, and Hazel shut her boot down with an extra flick of optimism. Perhaps this time would be different, she thought ambling over to join the rest of the group. For starters, ditching the wellies and investing in a smart pair of trainers could only be a good thing.

Audrey held a big 5-bar gate wide open and smiled as everyone poured through, her smile widening to a beam as Oliver tipped his hat to her, but then stern-faced, she gestured to Hazel to speed up. 'Come along, Hazel. No hanging back!'

Within ten minutes Hazel had managed to discreetly check everyone's choice of footwear, and her heart sank as she realised once again, she had got it wrong. All of the Tuesday Walkers were wearing actual hiking boots; sturdy, strong and with laces the size of small ropes, and unlike the natural-tan pop-socks Hazel wore, she saw thick woollen socks spilling out from the tops of them.

'How long have you been walking with the TW's?' Hazel asked an elderly lady with the energetic stride of a teenager and a gleaming mobile phone in her hand.

'A few months,' she answered, whilst checking her dazzling screen for about the tenth time in the space of a few minutes. 'I love these woods but wouldn't want to chase around them on my own. If you know what I mean.' She tapped her phone. 'Walking App. Never leave home without it.'

Hazel nodded, unsure she had enough breath in her body to continue the conversation and process what *one of those* was. Without any children of her own, let alone grandchildren, any mutual topic-possibilities between them soon dried up, and

Mrs P, mother to four and grandmother to thirteen, had now resorted to naming trees and identifying wild animal pooh.

It wasn't too long before Mrs P had increased her pace and Hazel found herself taking up the rear of the group. Soon the TW's were so far ahead, Hazel realised there was a very good chance she might lose sight of them altogether. No matter though, she decided – this was definitely the last time she would join them. She'd find another way to lose a little weight. And perhaps moving house would be a good idea too.

Hazel glanced up. Eerie black clouds were skulking across the sky to bully the last slice of sun from sight. She concentrated on replacing thoughts of being lost in the woods forever with the Victoria sponge she had made earlier; her planned treat for when she got home after today's walk. Hazel had asked Audrey if the group ever considered a nice little end-of-walk pub visit; a bacon-buttie or a cheese toastie and a mug of hot cider perhaps.

'Absolutely not!' Audrey had hissed through her teeth, in the same alarming manner as when she'd witnessed Hazel handing out toffee apples to trick-ortreaters, last Halloween. 'We jump into our cars,' she told Hazel, 'and then it's straight home for a hot bath.'

Soon, Audrey and her bath-loving TW's were almost out of sight, but as a splodge of rain hit Hazel squarely on her nose, she was still able to see the back end of the group put their hoods up in unison.

Hazel groped at her collar for hers. Oh, of course her jacket didn't have a hood.

A sudden squelch and the mud-caked forest floor sucked Hazel to a standstill. She looked down at her sinking feet. Her lovely new trainers with their soft turquoise panels were now chocolate brown with mud, and her snow-white laces all-of-a tangle with wet leaves and possibly wild animal pooh. The specific kind of wild animal pooh she would never know because the phone-wielding grandma was now very likely already back in her car and heading home for that hot soapy bath. Hazel sighed, feeling certain that not one of them would notice the too-plump lady, with the worst choice in footwear, was no longer still with them. Hazel imagined them jumping into their cars and zooming off home without a backward glance at the one unoccupied car left in the car park.

With some considerable effort Hazel managed to tug her feet free, from what surely must have been quicksand, and with her hands shoved deep in her pockets for warmth, continued on. This losing weight business was hard work and why were there no exit signs in a woods?

Having made two *questionably* correct decisions for left or right path choices, Hazel almost cried with relief, when a post with a red arrow painted on it, suggested she had chosen the right route to get her back to the car park.

The rain changed gear and moved from annoying wet stuff to the full-on soak your underwear kind. She put her shoulder into the wind and pressed on.

A hidden log had a different idea. Hazel's previously-turquoise trainers struck it with force, and she lurched sideways. Her hip did that clicky thing it does, and she fell to her knees again.

'Damn and blast it,' she said through gritted teeth as she sat waist-deep in slimy cold mud. But as much as she was hating being alone in the middle of a dense, and quickly-darkening, wood, Hazel was at least thankful that no one had been there to witness her falling over – especially Audrey.

Having tugged off some rather tricky ivy which had managed to loop itself around one of her feet like a wood-imps ankle bracelet, Hazel limped her way to semi-standing.

Panting, she stumbled over to the base of a huge tree whose trunk conveniently formed a half decent seat, and she shoved the strands of soggy hair from her eyes. Then realised immediately, she had now smeared mud all over her face. Could life get much worse, she wondered, leaning back against the damp scaly bark, and closing her eyes. She pictured making it home and rushing into her warm kitchen, where she would cut herself an enormous slice of Victoria sponge. She could almost taste the sweet raspberry jam and butter-cream filling that would melt in her mouth.

'Oh my word!' an urgent voice broke into her thoughts. 'What on earth has happened to you?'

Hazel's eyes snapped open, and she peered up through the sodden over-hanging branches at the tall man in front of her. 'Oh, you gave me quite a fright,' she told him.

'Gosh, I'm so sorry, but your eyes were closed, and you're completely covered in mud. I thought for a minute...' He held out his hand to her. 'Well, never mind. Are you hurt?'

'No,' Hazel pulled a piece of twig from her hair as she let him haul her to her feet, 'only my pride.'

He smiled and she grinned back at him. 'It's Oliver, isn't it?'

'It is, yes, but call me Ollie.'

'How did you know I was still in the woods?' Hazel asked, as they arrived back at the car park together. 'Did you see a car without its driver?'

'Well, no actually,' her rescuer said, the rain gathering in the brim of his hat like water in a moat. 'I noticed that you were no longer with us, just before the storm broke, and I told Audrey, I would head back to find you.'

'Well, I appreciate it,' Hazel said, unlocking the boot of her car. 'Thank you for rescuing me.'

'My pleasure,' *Call me Ollie* said. 'I'll see you next Tuesday then.'

'Oh, no. No, no. I'm afraid this walking business isn't for me,' Hazel confessed, lowering herself onto the edge of her car-boot to assess the damage to her trainers.

'Ah, okay, that's fair enough,' Ollie said, turning to go, and then stopped. 'Listen, I know we're both drenched, so this is probably a daft idea,' he added, removing his hat to tip the water away and revealing a head of thick silver hair, 'but there's a great little National Trust café just down the road. Do you like cake at all, Hazel?'

'Yes.' She nodded. 'Yes, I like cake very much.'

THE GOLDEN TICKET

'**N**ow stop this, Bryan Joseph Lansdale.' Mary reached across our table to slap my hand, as if I were a child halfway into a biscuit tin.

'Hey. Why are you full-naming me?' I asked.

'Because you've spent our entire lunch break moaning about a letter, and let's face it, Bry,' she paused to check the queue at the counter, 'it's not as if you're not used to rejection.'

I gestured towards the display of cakes. There weren't many this café didn't offer. 'Getting another one, are you?'

'Shouldn't really.' Mary sucked in her stomach. 'I've got that photo shoot for my book jacket coming up.' She flicked her hair back – a gesture I'd learnt, always came before she dropped her literary agent's name into the conversation. 'Harry Finn's been amazing, he's arranged everything.'

A cute waitress in skinny jeans, and cowboy boots, hovered nearby. I caught a whiff of her perfume: something fresh, but heady like a rose garden in June. I twisted around to offer her a smile – but she didn't want it.

'Did you see that?' I scraped back my chair and flopped my hands onto the table. '*Another* rejection.'

'What's this, Bry?' Mary looked at my hands and giggled. 'Do you want me to handcuff you and have you arrested for lack of pulling power?'

I snatched them back. 'It's easy for you to make jokes. You're happy. You've had *the* call. You've got *the* deal.'

'I was happy anyway, Bry. You know that. I have my lovely cottage, my cats and my health. The book deal was just the icing on the cake.' She glanced across at the queue again.

I scowled into my coffee. Mary was right. She hadn't needed a publishing contract to complete her. She wrote for fun. Whereas me, with two failed relationships and a puny one-bed terrace to my name, a publishing deal would be my golden ticket.

'Sorry,' I apologised – and meant it. 'I'm still struggling to get over that evil rejection letter, that's all.'

Mary gave an enormous sigh and stood up. 'I need another cake.'

I watched her point to a Danish pastry; oozing gooey apple that resembled baby food. I could smell its sickly sweetness from here.

The cute waitress swooped on Mary's empty, but chocolate smeared, plate and threw me a look. I imagined her thoughts. *Such a loser. A loser with a fat friend.*

'Come on then, Bry.' Mary returned with her cake – and another coffee. 'You just as well tell me which agent sent you the horrible letter?'

'It wasn't an agent – I'd exhausted my list, so I sent it to an actual publisher. He *said* he was open for submissions. Charles Nitwit, or something.'

Mary jerked the cake from her mouth as if she'd just spotted a patch of mould, and a splodge of pureed apple landed on her black shirt. 'He's *my* publisher, Bry,' she told me, a guilty tremble in her voice as if she were my wife confessing to an affair. 'His name is Charles Niblock.'

'Really?' My fists balled under the table.

'Yes, really.'

'What are the chances?' I shook my head – caught the waitress in my peripheral vision as she gave change to a guy in a suit *and* a free smile.

'He's ever so nice though, Bry. You must've just caught him on a bad day.'

'You think?' I watched Mary lick her fingers and wondered if they'd fit into the coffee grinder behind the counter. 'How long have I been writing for, Mary? How long?'

She licked pastry crumbs from her lips. 'Eleven years?'

'At least. And in all that time I've never received a rejection letter, more offensive and supercilious...'

'Oooh, I've had a *great* idea.' Mary brightened. 'Something that'll cheer you right up. Next Friday evening I'm doing a reading at the Wycliffe library, and...' she flicked her hair back, '...my agent Harry Finn will be there.'

'The 13th? I've got something on that night.'

'You should cancel it, Bry. If you bring your manuscript along, I can introduce you to Harry. Maybe he'll sign you too. The only thing is...' Mary paused as she spotted the apple on her shirt and tried to wipe it off. Made it worse. '...Charles will be there. You know the publisher who – '

16

'Yes, I know who he is. Thank you, Mary. I can't say I'd take any pleasure from meeting a man who told me he'd read more exciting prose on a Pizza Hut balloon.'

'Okay, fine. It's up to you.' She stood up with a huff. 'I'm just going to the loo.' She checked her watch. 'We're due back at the garage in ten. Best not be late, eh? My manager's a stickler for the time in his showroom – don't know about yours as you just wash the cars.'

I rolled my eyes, then searched the room for the cute waitress again. I spotted her stood by the door, holding it open for a man in a wheelchair. A sudden breeze swept her hair across her face, and I watched mesmerized as she pulled it back then held it together at the nape of her neck. Sara's hair had been that colour: not blonde, not red – but something in between. I wondered what she might be doing now. Married, divorced, still single like me?

Who knew? Who knew what someone did after they'd left their fiancé standing at the altar.

'Ready?' Mary was back and struggling with a sleeve of her coat that had turned inside out. I pretended not to notice. Where's Harry Finn now then Mary? I thought, zipping up my own jacket and heading for the door.

I studied my calendar as I took Mary's call. Friday the 13th. My heart beat a tiny bit faster. I'd been waiting for this.

'A lift? Oh, thanks for the offer, Mary, but I've got to get petrol on the way, and I don't want to make you late for your special night. I'll see you at the Wycliffe. Lots of luck.'

'Don't forget your manuscript,' Mary sang, 'and remember our plan: after my reading when everyone is chatting with their wine and nibbles, I'll casually introduce you to my agent – Harry Finn.'

'Sounds good. Thanks Mary.'

I stuffed the tools I'd selected into an old rucksack and headed out.

I glanced across at my manuscript lying on the passenger seat. The title page shone through its clear plastic wallet: Cloud Spotting. My best work to date. I thrust the key into the ignition with a snort. Stupid Charles Niblock. The man had zero taste.

Twenty minutes later, I pulled into the Wycliffe library's car park. Noisy gravel churned under my tyres as I found the last, but ridiculously small, space. I checked the time.

Excellent. Everyone should be in there by now. I retrieved my rucksack from the boot, full of any tools I'd thought might come in handy, and peered along the first row of cars for the swanky BMW, Mary had told me Niblock drove. If I could find Mary's battered old Rover, it would very likely be next to that. I crept along the next row of cars as the moon slipped out from behind a dark cloud to give me a little help.

And there it was. Niblock's car – black, shiny and pretentious.

The following morning, I groped for the ringing phone with an arm still heavy with sleep.

Could this be Harry Finn, I wondered, having read my manuscript? He hadn't wanted to take my hard copy from me, instead he'd asked me to email it to him when I'd got home – so of course I'd done it before retiring and sent him my number too.

So, was this him now desperate to give me the good news?

I took a deep breath filled with anticipation 'Yes. Hello. Bryan Lansdale speaking.'

'Hello.' The voice sounded familiar, but it wasn't Harry Finn. 'It's Tanya Price.

Mary's sister. We met last night at the library.'

'Um...' I glanced at my clock: 7.30. So much for my Saturday morning lay-in.

'You came in late and I found you a seat at the back?' she reminded me.

I heaved myself into a sitting position, pulling my pillow with me. 'Right. Yes.'

'Sorry to call so early but I thought, well, as you and Mary work at the garage together and all...' I heard her swallow, '... I thought you'd want to know.'

A sickening image of that last cake exploding Mary's poor heart in two filled my mind, and I dragged my fingers through my hair.

'Er, that's okay, Tanya. What's this about?'

'Mary was in a terrible accident last night. On her way home from the library. The police are saying one of her front wheels had worked itself loose.'

I caught my breath.

'I don't understand, hadn't she just got that old Rover of hers serviced?'

'Yes, she had, but...' her words dissolved into tears.

I waited a few seconds to be polite, then urged her to continue. *'But?'*

'She wasn't driving her Rover.'

'What?' I stared at the bulging rucksack in the corner of my bedroom. 'What car was she driving?'

'Her new BMW. She bought it with the advance from her book. I think it may have belonged to her publisher.'

'Charles Niblock?' I asked, hoping she couldn't hear my teeth grinding themselves into stumps.

'Yes, Charles, that's it. Lovely man. He wanted to up-grade, apparently, so he sold her his BMW for a good price.' Tanya's tears resumed, but I caught three muffled words before my phone slipped from my fingers and landed in my lap: 'life support machine.'

I leant over the side of my bed and threw up. The clear plastic wallet covering my manuscript, did little to protect it.

An hour later, I sat on the bottom stair, sore eyes fixed on my letter box. I planned to visit Mary as soon as the postman had arrived. Every day for eleven years I hadn't been able to leave the house until Reg had been. Luckily, he always came *very* early.

Footsteps approached, and I jumped up to open the front door.

A female police officer peered at her notebook and then back at me. 'Mr Bryan Joseph Lansdale?'

'Yes,' I said, unable to take my eyes from her cupid bow lips. 'What can I do for you?'

A male officer ambled over, and she waited until he was at her side before answering.

'This is Constable Murray and I'm PC Fane. Would you mind accompanying us to the station please, sir?'

'No, I can't. I'm waiting for somebody.' I stared at her, imagining her daily torment in having to wear such a stiff and serious uniform and not even a slick of gloss on those perfectly formed lips. 'I'm sorry,' I added, conscious that I was probably not making a very good first impression. 'I'm just waiting for – '

'Sir,' the male officer chipped in, his craggy lined face as dried out as the lavender bushes in my front garden, 'we need you to answer some questions concerning the attempted murder of Mary Francis Price.'

'Huh? What?' *But I didn't know it was her car*, I wanted to say – but didn't. Then as if the constable had read my mind...

'Cameras, Mr Lansdale.' A flash of a smirk. 'CCTV in the library carpark.'

I peered over his shoulder eager to see Reg with his mail bag.

'Alright, sir, have it your own way.' Constable Murray took a step towards me and began his well-rehearsed speech. 'Bryan Joseph Lansdale you have the right to remain silent...' even with the arrival of my postman he didn't miss a beat.

Reg ducked past me and tossed a large brown envelope onto my mat, then walked away from our little gathering as quickly as someone who had just left a stink bomb in a shopping mall.

Cupid-lips took me by the arm. She smelt like a vanilla pod. I didn't resist as she placed her small hand on top of my head and gently guided me into the back of the police car.

Then she doubled back to shut my front door. Thoughts of Mary clinging to life via a tube shifted to a far corner of my mind as I considered how considerate, as well as pretty, my capturer was.

'I don't like small spaces,' I informed the police officer shoving me into a room.

'No kidding and I haven't heard that before. Well, I suggest you start praying then, mate,' he said, handing me a blanket wrapped in cling-film. 'Because if that little lady in the Royal Shelbourne doesn't pull through – well let's just say you'll be in a small place for a very long time.' He began to close the door behind him, when I saw the same dainty hand, which held my head with such care earlier.

'Wait up, Frank,' she said stepping past him. 'I just want a quick word with your man here.'

'Sure, Em. He's all yours. But don't crowd him, eh. He suffers from claustrophobia.' I could hear his laugh bouncing off the corridor walls as he walked away.

'Take no notice.' She gave me a brief smile. 'Frank likes to wind up murder suspects.'

I swallowed.

'I brought this for you.' She handed me the brown envelope, which Reg had deposited with such speed onto my door mat. 'Thought it might be important.'

I slumped down on the metal bed, ripped it open and read through the first couple of lines. *Thank you for sending us your manuscript.... We are delighted to inform you....*

'Well?' Cupid-lips asked. 'Is it important?'

I slid the letter back into the envelope. 'Not anymore.'

THE LETTERBOX

'Roy? ROY!' Brenda's foot found her husband's shin and his eyes shot open.

'Are you asleep *again*?'

'What? No. No, I was only resting.'

'You look like a slab of haddock in the chip shop with all that newspaper draped over you,' Brenda snorted. 'Why are you so tired all the time?'

Roy lifted the Sunday paper off his chest, folded it neatly and placed it on the coffee table. It nudged Brenda's collection of Killer Sudokus and knocked them a little skew-whiff. Roy quickly straightened them. 'Well, that Laurel hedge was quite a job you know, and I'm not as young as I used to be,' Roy added with a chuckle.

'Well, you're going to have to move those bags.' His wife's stern expression remained intact as if she'd smeared on a face mask and couldn't allow it to crack. 'You know I can't shift them with my bad heart.'

'Right, right, of course. Your *bad* heart.' Roy eased himself from the sofa. *How many more years would she torture him with that?* 'I'll move them right away.'

'Yes, you will,' she confirmed, marching from the room, her orange mules clip-clopping on their new wooden flooring. Vacuuming a carpet had proven to be too strenuous for her *bad* heart, and the beautiful cream Axminster which Roy had laid throughout the house had to go.

Roy shuffled across the lounge. What happened to the girl he fell in love with? *My hero*, she used to call him, ever since the day he'd scooped her from the path of a cyclist. Now-a-days, the only time he felt like her hero was when she needed a spider caught from some corner – she was petrified of the things. He had to scour the house for them daily just in case she caught sight of one – with her *bad* heart.

Roy took the key to the patio door from its little pot on the mantelpiece – Brenda didn't like it to sit in the lock – security risk, she'd warned. He slid open the patio door, kicked his slippers off, and put his gardening shoes back on. He picked up two of the green sacks, he'd already loaded. *Who would believe one hedge cutting session could fill a dozen bags?*

Retirement – what a joke. He'd got more rest when he worked.

'Oh, and Roy...' Brenda took the corner from the hall to the lounge a little too fast and slipped quite spectacularly on her new Regency-Oak flooring. She grabbed the door frame and straightened herself up.

'Ooh, steady on there, dear,' Roy cautioned. 'Remember wooden floors have a lot more slide on them than carpets.'

'Yes, thank you Roy for pointing out the bleeding obvious.' She pulled her shoulders back and tugged the hem of her apron down. 'Oh, and just to remind you; Elsie is coming over tomorrow and she'll need a hand bringing all her boxes in.'

'Boxes?'

Brenda shook her head. 'Yes, boxes, Roy. Do I really have to tell you everything twice? Elsie's renting out her bungalow for a few months whilst she moves in with her daughter...'

Roy tried to join the dots, but Brenda's eye-rolling was blurring them into one fat messy blob of no-*idea*.

'Her pregnant daughter?' Brenda added.

Roy nodded his fake recognition to this additional info.

'Elsie doesn't want to leave any valuables in her house, so we're storing them for her.'

'Right. I'll clear a little space in our shed.'

'Good. Oh, and when you've done that, you promised to fix our letterbox, remember?'

'Letterbox?'

'Roy, you're giving me a migraine. I've told you about that damn letterbox a dozen times. When the wind gets up it rattles constantly and it's driving me insane. I knew it was a mistake to have it fitted so near to the ground.'

Roy held back the urge to remind Brenda, its positioning had been her idea. And that she had scoffed when he'd pointed out how inconvenient it would be for the postman and paper boy.

'You might want to speed up a bit,' Brenda gestured to the two bulging bags, Roy was still holding, 'the dump is only open 'till midnight.'

'Right you are.' Roy dropped the bags back down for a few seconds respite. They had felt as if they were doubling in weight whilst he stood there, almost as if an invisible pipe had pumped liquid cement into them. 'I'll have to bring these through the hall,' he called out, his back to her as he slid the patio door shut. 'Our bins are around the side; they'll block my route.' He felt Brenda's glare land like a bread knife in his back and turned slowly to face her. 'And I'm not sure that letterbox is *fixable*, dear.' He attempted a shrug, but his arms were too tired to assist his shoulders. 'We might have to buy a new one.'

'Don't be ridiculous, Roy.' Brenda's eyes crinkled menacingly, as if he'd just told her he was going back to sleep. 'Of course, you can fix it.'

'Why's that?' He grinned. 'Because I'm your hero?'

Brenda tutted. 'Don't be stupid, Roy, and make sure you say something to little'n over there,' she motioned towards the front door, 'on your way out.'

'Who? The lad across the road?'

'Yes, Timmy what's-his-name. He's doing another one of his tacky Table-Top sales right opposite *our* driveway. I don't want him still out there, littering the neighbourhood with his second-hand rubbish, when Elsie arrives tomorrow.'

Roy closed his eyes a moment, mentally checking that everything on Brenda's to-do list had stuck. Bags, dump, Timmy, shed... oh and letterbox. That was everything he hoped. Especially as he'd rather fancied watching a little of the BBC's Cricket highlights later. He glanced back at the other bags still in the garden and considered a bonfire, but a glance at Brenda's washing line, waving to him in the breeze whispered his answer.

He headed down the hall, hoping she wouldn't notice he hadn't removed his gardening shoes. But the heat from Brenda's stare as he passed her warmed the back of his neck, and he knew she had.

'I'll just put these in my boot,' Roy called, opening the front door, and hurling the bags and himself through it. He could see their neighbour's son sitting behind a long and cluttered table. 'I'll go and have a chat with Timmy, and then take a look at that rattly letter box for you.' He offered a smile, but Brenda seemed determined not to crack her mask.

Roy closed the front door behind him, and the letter box rattled in protest.

'Well, now, looks like you've found a sharp way to make a bit of pocket money here,' Roy said, beaming at Timmy's selection of bric-a-brac.

'Hey, Mr G.' Timmy greeted Roy with a high five. 'I was wondering when my best customer was coming over.' He rummaged in his cash tin. 'Piece of gum?'

'No thanks, Timmy. That won't work too well with my dentures. How's it going today? Have you sold much?' Roy glanced back at his house and spotted the upstairs curtain twitch. 'Um... are you thinking of packing up soon? Perhaps you would like a hand getting all this back into, er, your garage.'

'Not yet, Mr G. Dad says I can't store my stuff in his garage anymore; he's fed up of it getting in his way. He says I gotta sell *everything* this weekend – even if I have to sleep out here.'

'Oh, I see.' Roy took in the long picnic table with its assortment of broken toys and well-thumbed children's books. A skateboard and a pair of rollerblades poked out from a cardboard box on the ground.

'So, do you want to buy summit, Mr G?'

'I think I'm too old for most of this, but wow...' Roy darted to the end of the table to take a closer look at something that had caught his eye. 'Well, well, well. What have we got in here? May I?'

'Sure.' Timmy grinned. 'Go ahead, Mr G. Take a look.'

Roy carefully picked up the small clear container and peered inside. 'Why are you selling this fine chap, Timmy? And does it have a name?'

'Yeah, that's Henry. My Uncle Sid bought him for me, but Mum's scared stiff of it. Stupid really, 'cos if he bites you, it's no worse than a bee sting. He's only two years old, Mr G and they can live up to ten.'

'Really?' Roy stared at Henry's hairy brown and black legs. 'Up to ten years, you say?'

'Yeah. Which is good, but the females live loads longer than that. You can –'

'Ooh, nearly dropped him then.' Roy slipped the box gently back onto Timmy's table and turned to see who had startled them both by yelling his name. Roy saw Brenda leaning out of an upstairs window and gesturing for him to come back.

'Excuse me a sec, Timmy. My wife seems to want me.'

Roy darted back across the road to his own driveway and looked up. 'Yes, dear?'

'I've just had a look in the shed, and there won't be enough room for Elsie's boxes. So, you'll have to pack away that foolish train set of yours in the attic, and make room for them up there.'

The bedroom window closed, then opened again. Roy was still looking up, open-mouthed.

'TONIGHT.'

'Now, where were we, Timmy?' Roy asked. Having waited a moment to see if the window might re-open again, before heading back across the road to Timmy's Table-Top sale.

'I was saying you can have Henry for six quid, Mr G. If you want him.'

Roy opened his wallet. 'Gosh, I've only got a five pound note I'm afraid. Mrs G keeps me on a bit of a tight budget.'

Timmy took it from him. 'That'll do nicely – thanks.'

Still in its clear container, Roy carried his purchase carefully back across the road. He knelt in front of their letterbox and smiled at Henry. Then as he pushed the letterbox open with one hand, Roy gently coaxed the tarantula from its case with his other.

He let go and the letterbox rattled shut.

TAKE MY HAND

Headlights loom as a car ambles onto the bridge – the beam thankfully too low to pick me out. The sound of hollow tyres on thin tarmac. Electric perhaps. I force my spine against the rigid vertical column of the concrete girder – *let's merge* I will it. Make me invisible. My fingers curl tightly around the steel cables I'm holding onto. The car purrs past, without slowing. The driver hasn't noticed me. Unless they did and they didn't care. I exhale and release my sturdy companion. Time to look down.

The river is toffee brown and in places edged with litter, as if it were wearing a lacy collar. A gusty wind, biting and keen, is frothing the surface, but underneath

I imagine a current strong enough to pull me in and hold me there until it is over. Just like me and *him*. Over.

Footsteps. I snap my head around and see a woman on the bridge. A walker and her dog. And unlike the car's headlights, focused on the road ahead, not seeing me, not trying to stop me, *her* eyes lock onto mine. My heart sinks as fast as I hope my body will plummet once I step off this ledge; I've already registered the determination in the woman's eyes – she's going to make it her mission to stop me. I peer over the edge again, further this time, and now I can see even more of the river below me.

'Stop!'

The volume of her voice startles me, and I jerk back.

'Wait! Please wait,' she calls. Right behind me now. Looking up. Staring.

She has one hand holding her dog's lead, whilst the other grips the side of the bridge, as if she imagines it could shake me off, and she's helping to keep it still. I won't answer her, and she'll go away. My gaze jerks back to the river.

'Seriously! You need to wait,' she calls again, with an irritated insistence, as if she's speaking to a pestering child. *Put that biscuit down, or else.* Only I'm not a child.

I'm a 41-year-old who knows her own mind, and a mind that is well and truly made up.

I will jump.

I inch forward and lift one foot, ready to spring off the ledge. I've already figured out that is how I shall do it. When I'm mid-air I will need a little distance between me and the blunt iron structure of the bridge. I don't want my head to collide with any part of it, and knock me unconscious. That would be all wrong. I want to meet the surface of the river and feel it envelop me with its welcoming ice-cold arms.

'Hold on. Please!' *Her again.* 'Talk to me first.'

I lower my foot, but only because if I'd jumped then, it would have been to defy her wishes. No. That's not how it's going to be. It will be on *my* terms, *my* decision.

'Okay, I'll wait,' I tell her, 'until you're gone.' The woman slips to the ground and makes herself comfortable on the footpath. I watch her gather up her small dog and pull it onto her lap. She tips her head back against the railings, long waves of blonde spraying out from under a bobble hat, and she closes her eyes. She looks like an unconscious mermaid, waiting for someone to throw her back in the water.

A few moments later, the mermaid is awake and looking up at me again. 'This is Clark by the way. I named him after Clark Kent. He's a Labrador Retriever.' The woman's eyebrows disappear under the rim of her hat as if to say *So there – you will be rescued.*

'What, and some of his skills have rubbed off on you?'

The woman smiles. 'He's only a puppy. Don't expect much.'

I throw her a glare, working hard to fill it with contempt, but I like her. If this was a normal situation, say we'd met in a yoga class or something, we might be friends.

Another car comes past, and the woman draws her knees up to her chin. I'm not sure why – the car can't get her, the pavement's wide. Her dog wriggles free, but she tugs him back in with his lead.

'He's new,' she continues to feed me facts. 'My husband gave him to me last week. I didn't ask for one. I expect I'll find out what he's feeling guilty about soon. Do you have a dog?'

'No,' I say, something catching in my throat. 'No dog, no husband, no home and no life.' Tears spill, instantly becoming streaks of ice to sting my cheeks. 'You should leave,' I tell her. 'Nothing is going to change just by you hanging around to chat.'

She slid a phone from her pocket. 'Want to call someone? Or I can call them for you. Mum, Dad, a friend?'

'There's NO ONE,' I scream at her, and the wind causes a weird echo to bounce off the two central towers, as if the bridge wants to help me make her understand: *no one, no one, no one...*

'Well, just so you know, the second that you jump – and I mean whilst you're still free-falling like Spiderman without a web, I will be calling the Fire brigade to fish you out. And I'm a nurse, so I'll zip down the bank and do my darndest to breathe life back into you. And I have a good track record. Just saying.'

'The extremely muddy riverbank?' I ask, taking in her sharply pressed pale-blue jeans. 'I think you're bluffing.'

'Alright, I'll make you a deal,' the woman says, whilst she watches Clark cock its leg against the bridge as if she didn't realise dogs pee. She scoots sideways as the stream meanders towards her. 'If you give me three good reasons for ending your life – I'll give you three for living, and we'll see who wins. Okay? Fair? We'll take it in turns. You go first.'

I sigh. Loudly. 'If it means I'll get rid of you... then okay. One: I've lost my job.

Got fired in fact by my boss, who is also the man I thought loved me.'

Mermaid woman doesn't flinch. Has she heard me? She tips her chin upwards.

'One – the taste of a toasted crumpet. Hot and thickly buttered, with so much butter, that it runs down your fingers as you eat it, and you don't even care.'

I roll my eyes. 'Two: I lost my home and no salary equals – can't pay rent, and I've been living in a freezing, unlocked shed on an allotment.' A mist of warm air from my words cloud around my face as if to illustrate my point.

Nothing. No reaction, but I see her stamp her feet and tighten her scarf. She'll go soon.

'Two – watching a warm, golden, sunrise and...' she finds gloves in her pocket and puts them on. '...knowing you're alive to see another day.'

I look across the river at the dull-orange and gloomy-grey sky slipping below the horizon.

'Three,' I blurt, 'watching a sunset and thanking God it'll be the last one I'll see.'

The woman looks up at me on that one for a long moment, then gets to her feet.

'And Three,' she says, 'accepting a stranger's offer to come and stay with her, until we can find you an upgrade on your shed. Please...' she reaches her arm towards me, fingers twitching, '...take my hand.'

'No thanks,' I say, catching her dog looking right at me too. *Alright, Super Dog – back off.*

She drops her hand and consoles her dog with a nose rub. 'What was the job, you lost?'

'I *don't* want to chat. I'd like you to leave.'

'Last question then: are you sure it's completely over with the man?'

'He's staying with his wife.'

'Oh.'

That little ditty of info seems to have floored her, and she goes back to sitting on the ground again, despite the fact it is now raining.

'Stay then,' I tell her, 'if you want. But I'm going to jump anyway because that's what *I want*.'

'Would *he* want it?'

Good question. I remember Adam's expression – tortured, but resolute. He didn't want it to end, but he couldn't lie to *her* any longer. Broken – I hailed a cab and followed him home – not sure what I intended to do or say. Beg perhaps? Had I really considered doing that?

Stay out of sight, I'd instructed the driver, gesturing to a van we could park behind, then I'd watched Adam disappear behind his shiny red front door, with its weird knocker in the shape of an iron. Nursing my shredded heart, I stared at the house until the driver said he needed to get back. I hadn't found the courage to knock on their door – Adam's wife had won.

And now I'm here, and I don't have the answer to this stranger's question – but it doesn't matter anyway. It's too late.

'It's not too late,' she calls, making me wobble because it seems she's read my mind.

I blink rain from my eyelashes. *Please just go away.* Now my teeth are actually chattering, and her hand is on my leg. I hadn't realised she'd got that close. Her fingers in her wool gloves feel warm on my bare ankle – comforting even. *No!* I will not allow another woman to win.

The rain becomes heavier still, and I grope behind me for the pillar again. The bridge has become a boat in a storm and nausea rocks through me. I wish I was alone – this isn't how I planned it. I want to wrap my arms around myself – to get warm, but if I unpeel from this solid support, the wind may toss me over the side and that's not my choice either. The papers will report a natural disaster. An unfortunate accident. This will not be an accident – only *on purpose* can create the punishment *he* deserves. I glance down at the woman clinging to my leg; a human ball and chain. The wind is thrashing her face with her own mass of blonde hair, but with my leg in one hand and her dog's lead in the other, she must endure it. It can't be nice.

She says something else, but the howling wind snatches most of her words and tosses them aside too.

What if I went with her? Just for tonight. I could creep from her house at first light, come back and do this properly. Alone and without Mermaid Woman watching me.

'If you let go of my leg,' I shout, 'I'll get down.'

'You will? You mean it? It's not just a trick?'

'I'm trusting you,' I call back, 'so you'll just have to trust me.'

She let go, and I grab the cable which I'd used to pull myself up with, and drop back down to the pavement. Clark's paws thump against me, his tail wagging furiously as his wet tongue darts at my hands.

'Whoa, back-off, boy,' the woman says, pulling him away.

For a moment I think she might hug me – I'm surprised to find, I'm disappointed that she doesn't. We leave the bridge, with its flaking paint and rusting nuts and bolts, behind us.

'It's not much further,' she assures me, for about the sixth time since I'd asked if she had a car parked nearby. 'I hadn't planned on walking Clark as far as the bridge.'

'Lucky me,' I mumble, shoving my hands deep into my pockets. My fingers are refusing to thaw. If she hadn't have come along, I wouldn't have been holding onto to a stone cold pillar for over an hour. 'Would you really have climbed down the bank to fish me out?' I ask her.

'Probably.' She grinned. 'But I'm not sure I would have been able to resurrect you.'

'You make me sound like a vampire.'

'Ha, that's not the right word then.'

'Shouldn't you know the *right* word, being a nurse?'

'Ah well, that was a little white lie in the moment, I'm afraid.' We cross the road to a row of terraced cottages. 'I've always wanted to be one, but I'm actually just an ironing lady.'

'At least you've *got* a job.'

'Well, yes, and I really *love* ironing. So here we are.' The woman links into my arm as if she thinks I might bolt. 'This is us – the one with the shiny red door.'

KITTENS FOR SALE

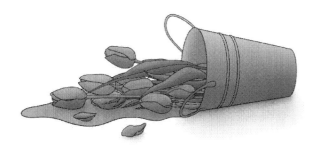

'There are five puppies to choose from, and the woman told me they're completely adorable. I thought perhaps we could go over later and take a little look?' Amy said, carrying her husband's coffee over to the table – although he wasn't a fan of her coffee, she'd at least made it today in his favourite mug. 'The woman said there's been a *lot* of interest,' Amy continued. 'Cesky terriers aren't often available.' She tapped her nails on the tabletop. 'Richard?'

'Not this again.' He closed his newspaper, then plunged his fingers into his hair as if he were demonstrating a shampooing technique, and sighed. 'You know my views.'

'I just want some company that's all.' Amy looked down at her nails – bitten and sore with angry cuticles. 'A puppy in our world. Can you imagine, Richard? Wouldn't it be wonderful?'

He folded his paper and tucked it behind a pot of pencils. 'Dogs mean trips to the vets,' he said gently, 'pet stores and worst of all parks. Deserted parks,' he added, as if *deserted* meant full of fire and guarded by the Devil himself. 'Why expose yourself to unnecessary risk?'

Amy realised he was looking at her hands and pulled them to her lap. 'I would be very careful.'

Richard scraped back his chair and went to the sink.

She followed him and slipped her arms around his waist, resting her cheek against his warm, solid back. 'Surely it wouldn't hurt to just have a little peek at them. You'll be right by my side?'

Richard twisted around, untangled her from his torso, and dropped a kiss on her head. 'I'm going to be late for work if I don't get a move on.' He tipped his coffee into the sink, and Amy watched the milky brown liquid swirl towards the plughole. It reminded her of the far-from-clear stream that had flowed through the bottom of their garden in their last house. Or was it the one before that? Married for less than two years, and yet they'd already moved four times. 'But I might think about a kitten for you.' He threw her a wink. 'They're a lot less bother.'

'Really?' Amy beamed. 'Thank you.'

Richard left the kitchen, then ducked his head back round the door. 'I nearly forgot. Can you get me a new toothbrush when you're doing our grocery order today? Mine's worn out.'

Amy leant back against the kitchen sink and gripped the work surface. 'I could pop into the village. The chemist will have a better selection.'

Richard's clean-shaven jaw tightened. 'Are you determined to make me late for work?'

'No.' She turned to stare out at the garden. 'I'll order you a toothbrush online with the food. Blue?'

'Yes, blue's fine. Thank you.' He disappeared into the hall, then came back again. 'You know how much I love you, right?'

She nodded. She did.

Amy jumped as the front door slammed shut, and realised her fingernails were in her mouth again. Even though she was certain that something dark and horrible was not hiding in the shadows down every alleyway in their village – Richard still managed to convince her of it every single day.

She rinsed out the sink with a sigh, glanced up and spotted the neighbour's black cat sitting on one of their seven-foot-high fence panels. Snowy white spots studded its coat, all the way to the end of its tail. It looked straight at her. 'If you were mine,' Amy whispered, 'I would call you Domino.' The cat seemed to sense her re-naming plan and sprang from sight.

'Right. The shopping.' Amy sat at the table and opened her laptop. 'Hate this,' she called out to nobody.

Snippets of news flashed across the screen as Amy waited for her supermarket page to open. Well would you look at that, she thought, peering at a picture of a celebrity couple announcing the arrival of their baby. The news isn't full of madmen lurking behind hidden doorways, waiting to plunge an axe through my head. I should call Richard and tell him. No need to keep me locked up at home after all.

Twenty minutes later, order complete, she signed out. The food would arrive on Saturday morning, as usual – when Richard would go to the door to receive it. As usual.

One last news bulletin slid into view, before Amy had chance to power down. A report which included the words *tragic death* reminded her of a newspaper cutting she had found shortly after her wedding day, on the 20th of December.

Newlywed and eager to please, Amy had gone up to the attic to collect their Christmas decorations, when a shoebox, labelled with her husband's late-wife's name, caught her eye. She had opened it, keen to get a glimpse of his previous marriage as Richard had offered her very little information. The newspaper cutting, she had found, filled in some of the gaps. A senseless stabbing, by a man, whose identity was eventually revealed as a known stalker, who'd up until then, had avoided being caught.

But Amy would never forget the look she'd seen on Richard's face when he found her reading the article. He crossed the attic beams and took it from her, placing it carefully back in the small box. Then he carried it away as if it contained an unexploded bomb. 'You don't want to read that,' he had said, his head disappearing back through the open hatch.

The screen on Amy's laptop went dark, and she closed the lid. That was the mistake she had made that day: *not* closing the attic's hatch-door behind her. But then why would she? She had been searching for tinsel and baubles, not for an explanation as to why the man she loved was perfect in every way apart from his over-protective nature. Back then, she could never have predicted how many times they would have settled in a house only to move again a few months later. Moves which had been bizarrely triggered by such insignificant incidents. A postman returning with a forgotten letter – *why had he returned?* A milkman whistling outside their front door at the crack of dawn – *why was he so happy?* Or the lad delivering their newspaper who, in Richard's mind, had seemed too old to be a *real* paperboy. All valid reasons for her husband to put their home up for sale and send them hurtling towards the next town on the map.

Amy looked around her kitchen, tired of her daily routine – and tired of the invisible rope that kept her tied to their current house.

A little April sunshine made an unexpected appearance and shot rays of dust-flecked light across the kitchen floor. Cleaned to perfection. Most days she had time to clean it twice. She went over to the back door, slid the three bolts, and unlocked it.

Stepping into the garden, Amy inhaled the green tang of their freshly cut lawn – mown by Richard of course. A visiting gardener would be out-of-the-question. She eyed their wooden back gate. A gate to freedom.

'Damn,' she said out loud. She'd forgotten to add a toothbrush to her order. She went back inside and reached for her laptop. 'No!' She shoved it away. She would go into the village and buy one.

Amy pulled on a jacket and tied her favourite soft scarf around her neck. She stepped in front of the mirror and took a moment to appreciate its colour: the vibrant pink of raspberry jam. When was the last time she'd worn it? She couldn't remember.

Only a ten-minute walk to the parade of shops, she thought striding out, and the best part – Richard would never know. When he brought in the bags from her on-line shop on Saturday morning, she'd simply slip the toothbrush into one of them when he wasn't looking. Wonderfully oblivious to the fact that his wife had enjoyed a trip into the village, and had savoured a small taste of life – beyond their home. Although she understood that his last wife had been the victim of a horrible crime, she still struggled to understand how he could possibly imagine that lightening, for want of a better word, could strike twice.

Nadler's newsagent was the first shop Amy came across, and she stopped to read the notices displayed in the window. A part-time volunteer was needed at the local RSPCA shelter. How incredible would that be, she thought, lifting her scarf to her face, now the sun had been shoved aside by a sharp wind.

She continued along the road. Walking past a Post Office without stopping to read their notices and increasing her pace as she passed a butcher's shop. Something about it gave her goosebumps. Hadn't there been a mention of a butcher in that newspaper cutting she had found in their attic? Or was it just a metaphor? She'd probably never know. Repeatedly asking Richard about the article had been fruitless, and his late wife's box of memories had vanished.

He may well have taken it from her before she had read it fully, but the headline had remained in Amy's head as solidly, and as permanently, as her skull.

Thirty-three-year-old Tania, wife of Richard Gill, found brutally murdered in supermarket car park.

Amy saw the chemist and went in. There were only two toothbrushes to choose from, but luckily one was blue. She hovered at a display of lipsticks. The sign declared: Live life to the full, with one of our new colours for Spring.

Amy paid for the toothbrush and left.

Hurrying back, she passed a florist, although hadn't realised until her foot collided with a bucket of pink tulips and the water gushed over her shoes.

'Oh no! I'm so sorry,' she told the man who rushed outside. He wore a knitted beanie, on what she guessed to be a bald head and along with his ears, had his nose pierced twice.

'It's totally not a problem.' He smiled. One of those smiles, she observed, that hit you straight in the eye and remained there for perhaps longer than appropriate. 'I probably take up too much of the pavement with all my buckets anyway. Folk bump into them all the time.'

'I seem to have broken a few of your tulips,' she told him, trying to bunch the damaged ones together. 'I wasn't looking where I was going.'

'Well, if you feel bad, then I'll let you buy them off me.

How's that?' He wiped his hands on his long canvas apron and went back inside. She watched him take his place behind the till. How would she explain flowers to Richard?

'Listen,' Amy said following him in, 'I'm happy to pay you but I shan't take any, thanks.'

'You don't like my flowers?' He looked at her as if she'd just refused to try his homemade lasagne. His gaze shifted to her raspberry-pink scarf. 'But look, they even match the colour of your nice scarf.'

Amy's fingernails found their way to her mouth, and she started to chew. Perhaps she could tell Richard a neighbour had brought them over, or she had just found them on their doorstep, and assumed they were a surprise from him. Amy realised the florist was watching her intently and she dropped her hand.

'Yes. Yes, you're right. They are a lovely colour. I'll take them.' The pierced man beamed. She hadn't refused his lasagne after all. But would they look like a gift, she wondered as she rummaged in her bag for her purse. 'Do you have any ribbon to tie them with?'

'Certainly. I've got all sorts here. Silky, shiny, silver, gold. Whatever you fancy. Now where did I put...' He began shuffling vases, pots and tubs of wire around. Then, just as he moved a box of scissors to the side, she saw it: a small card with a photo of a gorgeous tortoiseshell cat with pea-green eyes. Underneath, the words KITTENS FOR SALE were written in capital letters.

She picked up the card. 'Is this your cat?'

'Yeah, that's my Rosie.'

'Do you have any of her kittens left?' Amy asked, feeling a little out of breath as if she had just arrived somewhere that had taken her a whole lifetime to reach.

'Yep. All eight of them. They're out the back if you're interested in one.'

She nodded. 'I'd love a little peep. If that's okay?'

'Sure.' He shrugged. 'I'd better just flip this over though.'

Amy waited for him to turn his sign on the door to CLOSED, then followed him through a curtain of plastic strips.

The florist picked his way around the edge of the garden, which was more mud than lawn, and she did the same. They passed a toppling pile of empty crates stacked against a garage wall, and she felt herself cower slightly with the thought that they were about to fall on top of her.

'Here we are,' the man said, stopping so suddenly, she almost slammed into his broad back. They had reached a small wooden shed and she watched him crunch a large bolt sideways. He tugged the door open. 'They're in here.' He grinned. 'Take as long as you like.'

Amy rushed past him to a large paper-lined basket in the far corner. 'Oh, they're completely adorable,' she called. 'And hello Mum. You must be Rosie.' She knelt beside the basket of wriggling kittens and stroked a sleepy grey one. Its little damp nose brushed the back of her hand and Amy scooped up the tiny kitten. 'You're so so beautiful,' she whispered into its fur. 'I just might have to keep you.'

A voice behind her. 'That's exactly what I was thinking.'

SIX STARS

Doreen carried her dark-chocolate éclair, with its raspberry and vanilla-cream filling, over to her table.

It's a Tuesday, Doreen pondered, as her tongue caught the first taste of tangy raspberry. And *he's* here. There didn't seem to be a pattern. He could appear any day of the week really. Of course, sometimes she chose the wrong day and missed him altogether. Then, sadly, her week would lack a certain joie de vivre.

Doreen reached for the willow-patterned teapot and poured herself a cup of nice strong tea. She smiled across at Claire, the owner of the café, busily topping up her display cabinet. The éclairs took pride of place, whilst scones, cherry bake-wells and sugar-topped Eccles sat quietly in the background. Claire specialized in éclairs and although she sold the traditional kind, she also created some with unusual fillings and toppings. *Well, if they've named a cake after you*, Claire had confided in Doreen, *you just have to make it the star of your show.*

He put his paper down to take a sip of coffee. Doreen knew it was coffee – no teapot on his table, just a big manly mug. She watched him place it back down but keep his big manly hand around it. She wondered if she were to walk past his table and fake a small trip, if that big strong hand might dart out to save her.

He released his mug, looked up and treated Doreen to a smile. She returned it with the addition of a little wave. Then he went back to his crossword and that was that. He might not look up again. He usually didn't, although if he hadn't acknowledged her during his visit, he often gave her a polite nod on his way out, but never both, and his visits were always short; he was a very busy man, Doreen suspected. She'd learnt from Claire that he owned a garage a few miles away and sold second-hand cars: Ron's Motors. Doreen had thought about asking Claire if she knew if Ron was single, but he never wore a wedding ring, so Doreen felt she knew already.

Maybe she would go over and ask him the time. No – too random, and he may have noticed her watch. Doreen tried to focus on her grocery list. One small loaf, one lamb chop, garibaldis and two big oranges. She heard a chair scrape back – Ron was leaving. No eye contact – what she expected. Still now he'd gone she could nip to the bathroom.

Her cake had been delicious, as always, but it was a relief to wash her sticky fingers.

Doreen studied her reflection: greying hair, a saggy jaw and so many laughter lines, she almost wished she'd held a serious expression her whole life. Right, she thought, snatching a paper towel to dry her hands, there's no time to lose. She took her phone out and searched for *Ron's Motors*. If he wasn't going to strike up a conversation here, then she would just have to pay him a little visit on his own turf.

Decorated with length after length of multi-coloured bunting, Ron's Motors was much larger than Doreen had envisaged, as she wandered amongst the cars.

What a lot of money for a bit of tin and four wheels she thought, noticing the fluorescent *For Sale* stickers on each windscreen: £5,500, £7,250 and even £9,999. Shocking.

It wasn't too long before a man in a smart navy suit rushed over. He wore a badge that read RON'S MOTORS – CARS THAT LAST.

'Good morning, Madam. Gherkin's the name.' He offered his hand, and Doreen shook it. A chunky gold ring, with a decent-sized diamond in it, sparkled on the man's finger as he gestured at the cars. 'Seen anything you like?' He beamed at the selection as if he were presenting her with a basket of kittens to choose from.

'They're all very... lovely,' Doreen said, stumbling over her words. He wasn't who he was supposed to be. 'Is Ron here?'

'No, Ron's out on a delivery.'

'I see.' Doreen studied her shoes; her best tan ones with a bit of a heel to make her seem taller. 'I'll come back tomorrow.'

'Are you sure I can't help you?' he asked, sinking into his shoulders.

Doreen smiled. 'Yes, I'm quite sure, thank you.'

The following day, and with her tan shoes freshly polished, Doreen arrived at Ron's Motors once again.

This time, the man himself appeared at her side, as she stood admiring the vast selection of beautifully polished vehicles. He was taller than Mr Pickle from yesterday – she couldn't remember his real name – but not *too* tall.

'Hello there,' Ron offered his hand. 'I've seen you at Claire's, haven't I?' he asked, briefly placing his other hand over hers, before letting go.

'Yes, you have.' Doreen beamed, mentally pinning a gold star on Ron's lapel. 'I recognise you too.'

'Well, it's good to see you. What sort of car are we looking for?'

She thought of the prices. 'A small one.'

'Excellent.' Ron smiled. 'What are you driving at the moment?'

'I don't have a car right now.' She checked her shoes. 'My son has borrowed it.'

'I see, and what make is it, may I ask? A Ford, a Volkswagen...?'

'It's one of those People Rockers,' Doreen said, peeling back a strand of hair, the wind had whipped into her lipstick. 'It's far too big for me,' she added. She'd hoped to make him laugh, but he was just frowning.

'A People Rocker?' he repeated, his thick, well-groomed eyebrows knitting together. 'Ahh! You mean a People Mover.'

'Yes, that's it.' She nodded. 'One of those.'

'Right then,' he smiled, 'well, I think I may have the perfect car for you.' Ron walked her over to a Honda Jazz. 'It's such a *beautiful* shade of blue, don't you think?' he asked her.

Doreen's breath caught. He must have noticed the colour of her eyes, she thought, fluttering her eyelashes, and mentally pinning a second gold star on Ron's lapel.

'Yes, you're right.' Doreen nodded enthusiastically. 'It's a very pretty shade of blue, and a super little car.' She ran her hand over the smooth bonnet. 'I like it very much, Ron.'

'I thought you might. Now if I can have a quick look at your driving licence, then you can take it for a test drive,' he said, nudging his silver rimmed glasses up his nose. They looked familiar, Doreen thought. Yes, her late husband used to wear a pair almost identical. Bert had such great taste, so obviously Ron did too. Doreen smiled; *gold star number three.*

'I think a little drive out is a wonderful idea,' she agreed, 'but I'm sorry I don't have my licence with me today. Perhaps you could do the driving?'

Ron made sure Doreen was comfortable and buckled up, before clicking his own seatbelt into place, and they pulled out of the forecourt. Streamers of little coloured flags waved them off.

Twenty minutes later, and feeling quite relieved that she had been able to maintain her *interested* face throughout, Doreen now stood back on the bus stop waiting for her ride home. Ron had listed feature after feature as they'd whizzed through the countryside: amazing SRS airbags, incredible fuel efficiency and the oh-so-clever anti-theft system. The information had been endless, but there had been one thing she had been glad to learn. On their return to the garage, she had congratulated him on his safe driving skills, and commented on how lucky his wife was. Ron had thanked her for the complement, but he had no wife.

Gold star number four.

'I really think the first one we looked at,' Ron told Doreen on her latest visit, 'suited you the best.' They had just returned from yet another test-drive. This time, a neat red Clio, bigger than the white Fiat yesterday, but cheaper than the silver Skoda the day before. Ron had suggested today, they have a chat in his private office. 'You remember, don't you?' Ron prompted, and Doreen detected a hint of frustration in his tone, that she had never heard before.

Doreen fidgeted in her seat, her wool jacket a poor choice she decided, for such a warm day. Perhaps, she thought, after so many visits, she should offer to buy one of Ron's motors now. A shame though, because she'd thought they were really starting to get somewhere. Today, for instance, Ron had remarked on her new perfume, telling her she smelt nice. *Gold star number five.* She had clunked her seatbelt in place with a snappy pop.

'You're right,' Doreen finally said. 'The beautiful blue Jazz *was* my favourite.' She wondered if he'd ever admit to selecting it in the first place because the paintwork matched her eyes.

Ron held her gaze.

Doreen licked her lips and nodded. 'I'll take it.'

'Excellent choice!' Ron slid a multiple-page form in front of her, and she gasped.

'Oh, perhaps I could take this home to fill in?' She glanced at the door and wondered if she could still sprint as fast as she did when she was a school girl. 'I don't have a pen with me, I'm afraid.'

Ron found one in a drawer, reached for it with his large manly hand, then kicked the drawer shut. 'Now,' he said, handing the pen to her as if it were an ice-lolly, 'if you have *any* questions, just ask.'

'Yes!' Doreen dropped the pen as if it were burning her fingers. 'As a matter of fact, I do have one more question. *If* I buy your blue car, Ron, will you meet me at Claire's Café for a coffee next Tuesday?'

'For an eight thousand, nine hundred and ninety-nine, pound car,' Ron smiled, 'I'll even throw in an éclair.'

Doreen grabbed the edge of Ron's desk. 'Eight thousand and er... how much?'

Ron leant across and patted her hand. 'Doreen, I can take your People Mover in part exchange if you like? That's if your son isn't still using it.'

She took a quick glance around Ron's large office; four windows in total, but none of them open. 'I don't have a People Mover,' Doreen blurted.

Ron leant back in his chair and pressed his fingertips together. 'O.......kay.'

'And I don't...' she hesitated, wondering if she should continue. Ah, well, if she was making confessions, she just as well go the whole hog, '... and I don't have a son either.'

Ron sat up with such speed; she thought someone had shouted *Posture* in his ear. 'What? I don't understand.' He undid his jacket buttons. 'Can I ask *you* a question, Doreen?'

'Yes, Ron. Anything.' She gave him her best smile, which was hard when her best tan shoes were really starting to pinch after so much use lately.

'Doreen, can you even drive?'

'No, Ron.' She tried an eyelash flutter. 'I'm afraid I never learnt.'

She held his gaze, and he held hers.

The door flew open, and Mr Pickle came into the office. It suddenly felt a lot smaller.

'Boss,' he said, 'you're needed on the forecourt.'

'I'll be right there,' Ron said, answering his salesman but keeping his eyes firmly fixed on Doreen, and she thought Ron's nostrils were flaring just ever-so slightly.

Mr Pickle glared at her as if she were sitting in *his* seat. 'Er, no hurry, Boss, just when you've got time.'

'Well, it seems as if I've got plenty of time now!' Ron told him, shoving his chair back so hard, he nearly exited his office through the wall.

The following Tuesday Doreen, having switched her best tan shoes for her comfy flats again, entered Claire's Café. Ron wouldn't be there; she knew for certain, but Claire was launching a new éclair today – coconut and lime. She just had to come and try it.

Claire waved to her from behind the counter, her fuchsia-pink apron smeared in icing sugar and a new twinkle in her eye. Doreen waved back.

Then she saw him.

Ron, from Ron's Motors, sitting in his usual seat, with his newspaper folded on the crossword. Only today there was an extra place set at his table, with a pot of tea, an éclair on a plate and a neat white napkin, folded alongside.

Guessing – but more than that, hoping, it was meant for her, Doreen walked over to Ron's table and sat down.

She watched him place his paper beside his coffee mug.

'Claire's new flavour of the week,' he told her, nodding to the éclair – shimmering lime-green icing on top, with the fluffy white cream inside just visible.

'Have you tried one?' Doreen asked, pressing shaky fingers into her lap.

'Yes.'

'Oh, what did you think?'

'Well now Doreen let's just say, Claire's éclairs remind me of you,' he said, his expression as straight as a ruler.

Still angry – she guessed.

'In what way do they remind you of me?' Doreen asked carefully; although not looking forward to his answer: stodgy, sickly, or over-stuffed maybe?

'Very, very sweet,' Ron smiled, 'but once they're gone you always want more.'

'Oh.' Doreen beamed. *Gold star number six.*

TOO CLOSE

Ruth stood at her sister's graveside, her body rippling with cold shivers – part weather, part shock. She watched the pallbearers feed the strong canvas straps smoothly through their hands as they lowered the mahogany casket into the ground. Ruth heard Marie's coffin kiss the earth with a soft thud.

Clutching her blood-red rose, Ruth peered into the freshly dug hole. It was deeper than the usual six-foot, as the family had planned for the inevitable second coffin, her own, to be placed on top.

Ruth allowed the sweet-smelling rose to tumble from her fingers. Then waited. Waiting for what, she wondered; Marie to heave the lid upwards and whisper thank you?

But there would be no whisper from her. There would be no more words between them. No more late-night sisterly confiding's, no plans – the twins taking on the world. Not today. Not tomorrow. Not ever.

Ruth clutched Marie's scarf, now warming her own neck, and thought of the clothes the funeral director had dressed Marie in. A starched white nightie and plain, knee-high socks. Ruth closed her eyes against the memory of that last image.

Someone close by, her aunt she imagined, held back a sob, reminding Ruth that Marie's other family members were all lined up in a solemn row behind her. With her head bowed, Ruth stepped aside and glanced around, not seeing faces, only tight fingers gripping their own rose. Each of them silently waiting for their turn to step forward, and drop their flower into the gaping hole in the earth. Roses of yellow, white, soft-pink and peach, but none of them held a red one of course; red stood for deep, deep love – and no one could have loved Marie more than her own twin.

Ruth watched Alex, her youngest brother, step forward, then hesitate before allowing his yellow rose to fall alongside her own. Their father came next carrying his white rose. His limp more pronounced than usual, having left his walking stick at home. Pride Ruth suspected. Although he looked strong and upright for a man who had celebrated his sixtieth birthday only yesterday. He brushed Ruth's cheek as he moved past her.

Then came Aunt Elizabeth with her pink rose, her father's sister, and many years his junior. She stumbled forwards, her face so wet with tears, Ruth felt she should offer her a towel. After adding her delicate pink rose to the collection, she reached for Ruth's hand, unaware that her niece had overheard her whispering to a neighbour earlier: *I'm afraid our Ruth will die of a broken heart without Marie. Everyone knows*, she had added, *twins hate to be separated.*

Elliot walked up to the edge next, carrying his peach rose – tall, handsome, and confident. He paused on route to squeeze Ruth's shoulder. His concern managing to penetrate her coat – a gesture of best friend solidarity. Both Ruth and Marie had thought Elliot to be potential husband material once, but in the end the only company either of them needed was each other. Ruth managed a small smile as Elliot's sad blue eyes, sent his love all the way into her heart.

The vicar brought the funeral to a close with a few last words of comfort. Bowing his head, first to their father, then to Aunt Elizabeth, to Alex and to Elliot, then lastly to Ruth. Impressing on them one final time, that the Lord would watch over them all, as well as the deceased. Would he, Ruth wondered. Too late for His attentiveness now. Where was He during their eighteenth birthday party, when a happy day for two ended in a tragedy for one – where was his vigilance and watchful eye then? Ruth felt a scream surging through her body and clutched at her throat to prevent its escape.

The group were guided back to the waiting cars. Only a few more hours, she told herself and the mourners would be settled at home, moving on with their lives, and the gravediggers would be preparing for a good night's sleep. Their instructions, as always, to return to the churchyard at the first sign of daylight to fill in the hole.

Unbeknown to them that Ruth had gone back to the churchyard, climbed into the dark space, lifted the lid, and lay down beside Marie.

WHEN IN ROME

'Iris!' Leo appeared at the hatch and dangled a suitcase through the gap. 'This one?'

'Yes, the navy blue. Thank you.'

'I don't know why you bother,' he said, easing down the steps with her case.

She reached up to take it from him. 'You know why, Leo,' Iris kept her tone upbeat, 'traveling is one of the best ways to learn something about our world.' She dropped the case at her feet, then held her arms up to guide her husband back down the ladder.

'I'm okay. Don't fuss.' Leo jiggled his leg to shake her off. 'If you can go all the way to Europe by yourself, I can certainly make a safe exit from our attic.'

Iris leapt back; she knew how his foot felt directed at her ribs.

'Right, do you need anything else,' Leo asked, sliding the cover back in place with the end of a broom, 'or can I go and see to my dogs now?'

'No, just this.' Iris stroked her suitcase. 'Thank you.'

Iris placed the case onto her bed, making sure it sat squarely on the bath towel, which she'd carefully laid out to protect her lacey cream bedcover. Not a practical colour, she knew, but if your husband insists on sleeping with his three dogs in another bedroom, then why not make the room your own.

She took a breather. The case was already heavy, even before she'd filled it, but buying new luggage had become just another battle she had no hope of winning.

She heard a distant bark and moved to the window. Leo, with his woolen hat pulled down over his ears to keep the wind out, was making his way along the rugged coastal path. She could see Falcon his beloved Dobermann leading the way and his two retrievers, Pistol and Dash, chasing behind.

Iris smiled; she would have a good hour before he returned. Happily, she could ponder every outfit and accessory. As she unzipped her case a little flutter of excitement, like a lover's finger, ran down her spine. She fetched her red dress from the back of her wardrobe and folded the silky fabric into some tissue paper. Three shoe bags for three pairs of heels. Leo would definitely question why his wife of seventeen years would need those for a week's sight-seeing in Amsterdam. She found her good lipstick, the one that tasted of cherries, and dropped it into her toiletries bag besides her favourite perfume.

Everything packed. Everything hidden.

'Have a safe flight.' Leo patted Iris's head – with the engine of his old Jeep still running. It was so old in fact, it always surprised her that it ever started in the first place, but Leo refused to replace it. He didn't like change. 'I suppose I've got to pick you up again next week,' he grumbled, over the blast of a car horn which had pulled up behind them.

'Leo, you're parked in the taxi lane.' Iris rushed to the boot to retrieve her case. 'You know how crazy this airport gets. We should have used the Short Stay; we could've had a coffee together before my – '

'No need for all that,' Leo cut her off, slamming shut his boot. 'I've got things to be getting on with.' He did a playful patter of fingers against his back window, and Falcon, stretched out on his blanket, lifted his head in response. 'I hope you've remembered to pack your camera this time,' Leo called, ignoring the taxi driver's frantic hand gestures, and choice words, behind them.

'Camera?' Iris's eyes darted to her suitcase, concerned its thick navy panels had suddenly become transparent. 'Yes. Of course. But you know what a hopeless photographer I am.'

'Well, I won't argue with that.' Leo slid back behind the wheel, his door closing before she could reach it, and ending any possibility of a farewell hug. No surprise there, Iris thought; Leo hated public displays of affection – even on their wedding day, he declared hand-holding ridiculous just for some album they'd never look at again. He lowered his window. 'Remind me. Where did you go last year?'

Iris's heart pressed against her ribs. 'Lisbon.'

'That's it. You forgot to take your camera there. And the year before that – where was it again?'

'Um...' Iris closed her eyes, trying to remember what she'd told him. Was he quizzing her on purpose? 'Ah,' her eyes sprang open, 'Venice.'

'Yeah,' he scoffed, 'Venice. The only photos I saw of that place was a church steeple and a couple of pigeons and they were out of focus.'

She glanced around at the busy DEPARTURES entrance and stepped back onto the pavement. 'I'll try and do better this time.'

'Well see that you do. I expect to see windmills, not just one flippin tulip from Amsterdam.' Leo sent his window up, and much to her relief and the queue of drivers behind him, he pulled away.

Inside the terminal, Iris checked her ticket. Fiumicino Rome. Window seat. Her guidebook to Amsterdam, safely stored in her luggage to read through and make notes on her flight home. In a way, it was sad that she couldn't share that this was her fourth trip to Rome; but then Leo could never find out the appeal Rome held for her.

She passed through security without a hitch and found a table in her usual airport cafe: FlyAway, and beamed at the waitress placing a bowl-sized cappuccino in front of her. As Iris tipped a little sugar into the chocolate-dusted foam, she recalled a conversation with Leo on her return from her very first trip to Rome.

'I think I'll go to Madrid next year,' she had casually announced as they sat in the garden; the sound of waves thrashing against rocks, her constant soundtrack. 'I'll be able to tell you all about its famous stadium and glorious parks.'

Leo had complained that she was wishing her life away, talking of next year's trip only hours after she'd returned from Rome. 'It could be so good for us though,' Iris had insisted, 'if I go and explore a different city every year, it'll give us something new and exciting to talk about.'

Leo's bottle had thudded onto the patio slab with a crack. 'Why do you want to go galivanting around a load of foreign countries, Iris? What's wrong with just reading a good travel-guide?'

A guidebook! And the idea was born.

No need for a trip to Madrid the following year – she could return to Rome.

'It's not my fault that you won't leave your dogs to take a holiday – even one in this country,' Iris had added. Which was a mistake.

Even the postman had seen through her carefully applied concealer.

Once settled on board, Iris picked up the Emergency-procedures card, and as a courtesy to Leo, read it in full. In all the years, they'd been married she had never been able to persuade him to do anything that involved getting on a plane. His obsession with aircraft-disaster stories was beyond absurd. Flying didn't bother her, but she always kept her seatbelt securely clamped across her lap throughout the entire flight. That would please her husband, she thought, even if nothing else did.

The flight was smooth – the only turbulence, the flutter of butterflies in her own stomach. Iris twisted in her seat to peer through the small oval window and study the clouds. As soon as the plane dropped below them, Rome, in all her glory, would come into view. Even the air smelt different there, with the nutty aroma of Italian coffee, vanilla-scented gelato and smoky roast chestnuts, replacing the ocean's salty odour and swampy-stink of wet seaweed of back home.

The captain's voice filtered through; a beautifully warm September's day was waiting to greet them in Italy's romantic capital. How wonderful. Of course, it couldn't be any other month of the year because Gianni was only allowed this one specific week off from his job as doorman at the Hassler. The Hassler, perched at the top of the Spanish Steps was, in Gianni's opinion, the most prestigious hotel in Rome, and he was happy to follow their rules.

Iris's room on the sixth floor, the same each year, looked over ancient roof tops and dome-crowned churches. And during sunset, the view became even more breath-taking. Bliss.

The plane juddered and Iris felt the wheels meet the runway with a rubbery screech. Across the aisle a baby in its mother's arms began to cry, and Iris's bag tipped over at her feet. She leant forward to rescue its spilt contents. Glancing back at the baby, now soothed and smiling, she swallowed her sadness – another lost battle.

Sunshine pierced Iris's window as the plane crawled to a standstill, and she closed her eyes as she released her seatbelt. For one week she could live another life. If only she had the courage to make it permanent.

Iris's suitcase circled to her side, and she tugged it from the carousel.

'Ah, that's clever!' A woman next to her acknowledged, nodding at the length of tartan ribbon that Iris had tied to the handle. 'A very good idea. I wasn't sure if that one was mine. They all look the same, don't they?'

'They do, yes,' Iris agreed, remembering her words to Leo.

I'm adding a bit of tartan ribbon to remind me of home. Just in case, she had tried to disguise her nervous laugh, I decide not to come back.

Leo didn't laugh.

Iris sped through the exit doors – Nothing to Declare. She was moments away from being welcomed into Gianni's open arms, and the start of a whole week of freedom from the routines of life back home – dull and repetitive as the perpetual tide, only meters from her front door.

She paused to tuck a loose curl behind her ear and scan the expectant faces. Gianni usually got her attention by shouting her name and waving a red rose above his head. Iris! La mia bella. Today, though, everyone seemed to be shouting, and some were gravitating towards a large television screen, positioned high on the wall above the ARRIVALS sign. The News channel blared out. Not that she spoke Italian – she wished she did. But underneath the pale face of the newsreader, English subtitles ran along the bottom of the screen.

A Dutch airline, with a previously untarnished record had crash-landed upon its arrival in Amsterdam. It had left Aberdeen almost the exact same time as her Alitalia aircraft had left for Rome. The scene flashed up of a plane, barely visible behind a curtain of black smoke. Iris's hand flew to her mouth as the footage showed ambulances and fire engines circling the flames.

All around her people were pressing mobile phones to their ears. Like her, she imagined, horrified to learn of the tragedy, but equally relieved that they had arrived safely here in Italy.

The English subtitles continued with the addition of a helpline – a number for family and friends to call.

'Leo,' Iris whispered her husband's name. He would see the news and think that was her plane – her destination. She would have to call him and tell him she was safe. But then she would have to explain everything: the fake destinations, the truth and the lies. She imagined returning home, to Leo and the consequences.

A voice she recognized called her name.

'Iris! La mia bella!'

And she turned to see a red rose held high above the mingling crowd. She waved back and made her way towards Gianni. Iris inhaled, determined to enjoy the moment she fell into his outstretched arms. She would take strength from this one glorious moment, before making her last call to Leo.

THE PORK PIE

'You spend more time at sea than a turtle,' Nina told her sister with a playful glint in her eye. 'I'm surprised *you* haven't met a nice man on board yet.'

'That's because I'm not looking for one,' Lois said, crooking her little finger as she lifted her teacup. 'Besides, the *gentlemen that cruise* are more interested in how much food they can devour during each twenty-four-hour buffet, than...' Lois paused to sip her tea, '...seeking out a fifty-year-old divorcee for a game of bridge on deck seven.'

'I'm sure you're right.' Nina nodded. 'I've certainly met a few recently, who made it very clear, they preferred cheap fast food over fine dining given the choice.'

'Well, I blame that agency you're with.' Lois frowned. 'What's their name again?

Breaking Hearts?'

'No.' Nina chuckled. 'Hearts on Sleeves.'

'Ah yes, that's it. Are they still sending you off on those awful dates?'

'You make me sound like a serial dater.' Nina took a triangle of lemon-scented shortbread and nibbled the corner. Grains of zingy citrus burst on her tongue. 'And you were the one who signed me up with them, and listed my requirements, remember?'

Lois smiled. 'I did. Guilty as charged. I just want you to find a really nice man this time, that's all.'

'And by nice you mean rich.' Nina glanced around the restaurant for the waiter.

Lunch had suddenly become exhausting.

Lois laughed. 'Nice *and* rich – the perfect combo. You deserve it after...'

'Let's not bring John into this, Lois.' Nina snatched her handbag from under her chair and plopped it onto her lap. 'We were happy.' She spotted their waiter, and did a quick charade of pen in her fingers and signing a bill. He nodded his understanding and she wondered if waiters and waitresses found the universal mime helpful or rude. *Or* perhaps they were just pleased not to have *Oy you!* shouted across the room at them.

Lois leant in. 'You could have been *happier* if he'd managed to sell one of his paintings once in a while.' She sat back with a jolt. 'That's all I'm saying. Anyway let's not argue.'

Their waiter arrived with the bill and Nina opened her bag to retrieve her purse. He went to leave, but Lois had the cash all ready for him and thrust it in his hand.

'Keep the change,' she purred.

'Hang on,' Nina tried, but Lois threw her a stern look.

'This one's on me,' she said. 'It's the least I can do when I'm about to desert you for a month-long cruise.' Then she shook her head and giggled as if remembering something funny.

Nina sighed. 'What now?'

'I was just thinking about that last date you went on.' Lois pulled a pained expression. 'Gerald, was it?'

'Gareth,' Nina corrected. 'Gareth the undertaker. He smuggled me into a post-funeral reception for our lunch.'

Lois roared. 'That's it! Unbelievable.'

Nina smiled at her sister. 'Well, I've been trying to erase *that* date from my memory, *and* the one before him. Alan, or was it Adam? Anyway, all I can remember is that he produced some two-for-one vouchers, and then bragged how happy he was to take me out for free.'

'That's shocking.' Lois clutched Nina's hand dramatically. 'You deserve to have sizzling Saturday night's out, and a man who can collect you in a vehicle with four wheels and a roof!'

Nina pressed her lips together. She wouldn't react to another of her sister's sneaky digs at her late husband.

Lois paused for a moment, before scraping back her chair and draping her jacket over her shoulders. 'Well, I give you permission to quit that agency.'

'Oh, I'm going to,' Nina reassured her big sister, 'and I'll do it today.'

That evening Nina clicked off the TV and picked up her book. Then put it back down.

The lure of her open laptop, its little green light winking at her from the corner of the room was too tempting. With a weary sigh she logged onto Hearts on Sleeves. Her sister was right – it was time to withdraw her profile. There were no nice men out there.

Nina nudged the computer's mouse and dipped the cursor into the Remove Profile box, but the message bar suddenly obscured it. One Un-read Message it declared.

Oh, she thought, well it would be rude not to read it.

An invitation sat waiting for her from Donald Donaldson. A fake name surely?

Although, she reflected, she too was guilty of a name disguise. Lois had set up her profile as Abigail – far more intriguing, she'd suggested, than Nina.

Perhaps Donald Donaldson would be the very man her sister would whole heartedly approve of. Nina sent a quick reply, before she could change her mind.

Yes, she would be delighted to meet outside the François Brasserie in Old Market Square. Thursday at noon. How lovely. Mr Donaldson obviously had taste; François's had to be the most expensive restaurant in the area. Nina had never been. To go, even once, would be a dream. Hearts on Sleeves seemed to be taking her sister's wish list seriously at last. No more cheap dates.

Nina climbed into her taxi – a pre-paid treat from Lois – and smiled as they pulled into Old Market Square at five minutes to twelve. Nina had spotted her date standing outside the François Brasserie holding a beautiful bunch of yellow roses. He wore a cozy-looking chocolate brown coat and he looked *nice*.

'Hello, Donald, I'm Abigail,' Nina said, offering her hand, and being immediately drawn to his big smile and twinkly, honest looking, blue-grey eyes. She had a sudden urge to blurt out that her name was actually Nina.

'Call me Don,' he said, shaking her hand with the uneasiness of someone meeting their new boss for the first time. 'It's lovely to meet you. And *thank you* for coming.'

'Of course.' Nina took a quick little look into François's, and saw a free table right in the window. Reserved for them, perhaps? 'Why wouldn't I come?'

'Ah well, not everyone does. Let's just say Hearts on Sleeves don't always get it right.' He grinned. 'I have high hopes for today, though.'

'Yes,' Nina agreed, catching a waft of roast garlic as a couple stepped out of the restaurant holding hands and smiling, 'so do I.'

'I thought we could wait over there for a moment.' Don gestured to a bench further along the pavement. 'We have time.'

Oh, we must be early, she thought, going along with his suggestion, and following him to the bench. Nina eyed the gleaming black paintwork, as they approached, wondering if it were dry, then she slowly circled the entire bench. She had to check that she hadn't missed any *wet paint* signs looped over an arm or hanging from the back. A nasty experience in a park once, involving a freshly painted red bench and her best white trousers, had left her suspicious of every public seat since.

'Oh, it's quite dry,' Don told her, spotting her ritual. 'It hasn't rained for days.'

'It's not the weather I'm worried about,' she said, ignoring his bemused look. She nodded to the flowers he was still clutching; a dozen perfectly formed rose buds, the colour of lemon sherbet. 'They're beautiful. Are they for me?'

Don glanced down at them as if he had forgotten they were there.

'Oh, no. Sorry,' he apologised. 'These are for my mum.'

Nina clutched her chest because her heart rate had just doubled. 'Your *mum* is joining us for lunch?'

Don smiled. 'No, I'm afraid not.' He held Nina's gaze as if he were studying the colour of her eyes. 'She died many, *many* years ago. When I was ten actually,' Don added, running a finger gently over a bud. 'The cemetery, where she's buried, has been closed for repairs since before Christmas and has only just opened its gates again.' He gestured to the bus stop over the road. 'There's a Number Nineteen due in,' Don checked his watch, 'seven or eight minutes. It's only about a ten-minute ride.'

'So, we're not having lunch at François's,' Nina asked, hearing the disappointment in her voice and feeling quite ashamed of herself. 'Perhaps we should do this another time,' she added, as they crossed the road to join the queue at the bus-stop. 'I mean as you obviously have things to do.' She heard her sister's voice in her head: *Run Nina. Run for the hills.*

'No, no. Not at all. It's just that the church is very close to this lovely little place I'd planned to take you for lunch. I thought two birds with one stone, and all that.' Don chuckled at his own joke as the Number Nineteen rumbled to a halt in front of them.

Nina sighed as the double-decker obliterated her view of François's – a restaurant, she now knew, she would never sample the menu from.

'Top deck,' Don announced, leading the way. 'We'll be able to see everything from up here.'

Nina gripped the handrail as she cautiously climbed the narrow staircase behind him. Had someone opened all the windows up there, she wondered, as a sudden cold breeze whipped her hair out of place.

'Ah, it's an open top bus,' she exclaimed, following her date to a row of empty seats right at the back.

'It is, yes.' Don grinned, wiping his sleeve across a rain-splattered vinyl seat for Nina, then gesturing for her to sit down. 'Fun, eh?'

Nina thought it best not to answer and gazed out at the view instead. As the bus jostled for its place in the traffic, she saw a man with a bulging rucksack. Wobbling along on a rusty red bike, he reminded Nina of her John. Always having to cycle to any potential customers – without the luxury of a car to keep his paintings safe.

'So, do you not own a car then, Don?' she asked, a few minutes into their journey.

'No, only a push bike. You?'

'No, I've never learnt. To drive that is,' she added. 'I can manage a bike quite nicely.'

'Oh, watch out for that branch,' Don warned, as the driver took a corner too fast, and skimmed a row of trees. Nina lurched forwards and thrust her head to her lap, in emergency-landing style. 'It's okay.' Don patted her back. 'All clear now.'

She sat up slowly, assessing any damage to her best coat, but appreciating his offer to switch seats.

'The hazards of the top deck, I'm afraid,' Don chuckled, flicking a broken twig from his shoulder. 'But you really do get a good view from up here,' he added, turning back to her. 'People's gardens, unusual chimney pots,' he paused to lean in and pick a leaf out of her hair. He grinned. 'And the *tops* of trees.'

'I guess you're right,' she conceded, unable to not smile at his enthusiasm.

Soon the bus made its first stop. No sign of a church, she noted, but they were parallel to a cinema, announcing its current film in neon lights. Nina jerked her head back and blinked.

'Do you not like going to the pictures?' Don asked.

'Oh, no. It's just that the lights were in my eyes.' She smiled. 'I actually enjoy going to the cinema very much.'

'So do I,' he said, slapping his knees with obvious joy at their shared interest.

'Perhaps we could go together sometime.' He held onto the bar of the seat in front as the bus lurched onwards. 'Tuesdays are always a good choice.' He wriggled excitedly. 'It's two tickets for the price of one.'

Nina imagined Lois's reaction, and she tugged her scarf to her throat as another whoosh of cold air swallowed her face.

One more stop and Don led the way down the twisting metal staircase and off the bus.

They crossed the road to the church and entered through a squeaky gate.

Nina tottered along the gravel path alongside Don Donaldson, trying not to think about the scratches that were no doubt ruining her best black heels.

'Ah, here we are,' Don announced, pointing to an angel-guarded gravestone, and surrounded by a lot of long grass. 'This is Mum.'

Nina read the inscription as he disappeared to fill a vase with fresh water: Violet Ann Donaldson. She smiled; so, he hadn't made his name up then. Oh, but the date.

She checked it again. Yes, it was today. Violet's birthday.

Don reappeared. 'Well, the tap is working again. That's something, I suppose,' he said, kneeling at his mum's graveside to position her roses.

'I'll just wait over here,' Nina said, stumbling back a step. 'Give you a moment.'

She walked over to the mossy church gate and waited.

A few moments later she saw Don gently kiss the top of the stone, before picking his way back through the miniature garden plots.

'Thank you for that,' he said, taking Nina by the elbow, and leading her back into the street. 'Now, how about that lunch I promised you?'

The Cacao Nib Café looked inviting, and Nina thanked Don as he held the door open for her, not just for his chivalry but for his good taste too. A warm, yeasty smell of home-baked bread hung in the air, and a glass-fronted cabinet caught Nina's eye as soon as they stepped inside. A carrot cake smothered in buttery icing and decorated with little carrots made from bright orange marzipan, took centre stage. There were plenty of savoury choices too, including scotch eggs, the size of tennis-balls and cheesy-topped, deep-filled quiches, garnished with bunches of watercress and plump pink radishes. Everything, in fact, Nina decided, just screamed *eat me*.

'The food looks wonderful,' she gushed. 'Have you booked us a table in that gorgeous little courtyard out there?'

'No,' Don said, in a hushed voice, 'it's better value to opt for a take-a-away here.'

'What?' Nina felt her knees give a little.

'Don't worry,' he reassured her, 'there are some picnic benches just a short walk from here, with a fantastic view of the river.'

Nina glanced down at her shoes. 'Right.'

Armed with their choices, which included ham and chutney baguettes, sausage rolls and banana cake (Nina had desperately wanted the chocolate gateaux but had to think about her best coat) they made their way across a leafy park, and up a slightly steep hill.

Nina eyed Don's chosen bench suspiciously.

'It's okay, Abigail,' he reassured her, sweeping his hand across the seat, 'I don't think these have been painted since the end of the war.'

She sat down marveling at how he had known that was her fear. The view of the river was indeed *fantastic* and so was the conversation – Nina couldn't deny it. But an hour or so later, shivering as they waited for their return bus, she knew that if he asked her for a second date, she would say no. Sadly, the man was too much of a bargain hunter. Lois would never approve.

Nina had only just come through the door and taken off her coat when her phone rang.

'Hi, Lois. Are you all packed?'

'Never mind my packing. I want to know how your date with Mr Donaldson went today?' She giggled. 'I do hope that agency got it right this time.'

Nina sunk onto her sofa and sighed. 'Well, he was a *nice* man, but we didn't have lunch in the François Brasserie,' Nina told her sister, removing her shoes with her free hand, and rubbing her feet.

'Talk me through it,' Lois demanded.

I need a cup of tea, Nina decided, padding out to the kitchen, and taking out her frustration on the kettle by directing the water through the spout at full force.

Having listened to her sister's advice: *Quit that agency, now!* Nina's efforts to *Exit* had ended up in her reading just one last message again.

And really, what *were* the chances of Lord Boving being an actual Lord?

The following week – and a Saturday night – Nina lifted her collar against the wind as they left the warmth and sparkle of François's behind them. The restaurant had certainly been all that she had hoped, but sadly the company not so. It turned out that Lord Boving really was a Lord, but unfortunately, he also had all the attributes of a titled, rich man who knew he was a titled rich man. She would remain single she decided, and that was just fine.

Together, they walked through a cobbled alley. A short-cut to a quiet cul-de-sac, Lord Boving had informed her, to where his driver was waiting to take them home. To avoid twisting her ankle in her heels, Nina concentrated on choosing the flattest cobbles to walk on, which provided a nice distraction from her date's constant boasting.

Half-way along, Lord Boving, or Lord Boring as Nina had re-named him in her head, stopped abruptly as something in a shop window caught his eye, and she crashed into his shoulder.

'Gosh, sorry,' she apologised.

'Did you see that?' he asked, pointing to a tray of Danish pastries displayed in a delicatessen's window. 'There was a fly on one of them just now.' Lord Boring's moustache quivered with disgust. 'I've a good mind to go in there and ask them what they think they're playing at.'

But Nina wasn't looking at the Danish's. Instead – she had spotted a large golden crusted pork pie, sitting on a plate, and surrounded by dozens of cherry tomatoes. A tiny card stabbed into it with a cocktail stick, read: One tray of cherry tomatoes FREE with every purchase of a large pork pie. That's quite a bargain, she thought smiling to herself at the thought of Don Donaldson's kind eyes twinkling with pleasure. In fact, she decided, that pork pie could make an excellent shared picnic for two, sitting on a park bench – perhaps even a park bench with a view.

Lord Boring puffed his cheeks out. 'I don't believe it,' he said. 'You're smiling? Am I to assume that you think this establishment's lack of hygiene is actually funny?'

'Oh no.' Nina shook her head. 'That's not what I was thinking at all.'

THE TREE

I caught the look on Tom's face, pinched and anxious, as he pulled over. He didn't want me to get out of the car. Neither did I. We were two streets away from Mistletoe Lane, and the home I shared with Jason. I wished it were more. I wished it didn't exist.

'I'm not sure about this, Lizzy. I still think we should do it together.'

'No,' I shuddered at the thought, 'that could get ugly. I'll be fine.'

Tom buried his face in his hands and nodded. 'God, I hope so.'

I stared at his long, slender, gentle fingers that earlier had teased my hair and played over my lips. Fingers, belonging to the man, I had decided, I could no longer live without.

'You should make him some coffee first,' Tom said, sliding his hands to the steering wheel and gripping it hard. 'To dilute the alcohol.'

'Hopefully that won't be a problem tonight. It's Tuesday after all and he has work in the morning. He'll have a couple, but that's probably all. Plus, he won't be expecting this,' I added, trying my best to soothe Tom's nerves, 'and Jason can't deal with unexpected information. He just freezes when he's surprised. So, I have *that* on my side.'

I un-clipped my seat belt and pulled my shoulders back. 'I'm just going to tell him that I'm leaving him and go. He won't have time to process it or even *begin* to make one of his punishment plans.'

Tom shivered. 'Alright. If you're sure.' His finger brushed my cheek. 'I'll be waiting right here for you.'

'Thank you.' I tapped his knee and pulled a silly grin to lighten the mood. 'And if I'm not back within the hour, it's all gone horribly wrong, and he's buried me under the patio.'

Tom's face turned deathly white, his eyes staring in disbelief.

'God, sorry. Sorry! That was a stupid, stupid thing to say. A bad joke.' I pulled a pleading expression. 'You know I make terrible jokes when I'm nervous.'

'I know.' He reached into the back seat and passed me my coat. 'Just go. I'll see you soon.'

I nodded gratefully as I got out of the car and blew him a kiss.

I checked my watch as I let myself in. I'd been gone two hours, thirty-five minutes. The perfect amount of time. Not too short that an evening with friends discussing our latest book wouldn't be believable, but not too long that my lump of a husband could get himself completely legless. Although usually, the drunker he was the fewer questions he asked. *But* it's Tuesday I reminded myself.

I left my keys on the hall table, having had duplicates already made so I could return tomorrow, when Jason was in work, and collect the rest of my belongings. I made my way through the house, doing my best to put a bright, casual smile in place. I thought of my packed case hidden in the spare room, and glimpsed my future with Tom – safe and loving. A little courage trickled through me. *This was the night.*

A loud scrape of a garden chair told me the lump was outside. I kept my coat on and slid open the patio door. The living-room light threw a warm, but eerie glow, over the chaos. Like a rapid spread of chickweed, empty beer bottles seemed to have taken over. Some lay in broken pieces on the lawn where Jason had tossed them, even more were lined up on the small garden table and of course, there was one in his hand. He jerked it to his lips when he saw me. A defiant swig and a glint in his eyes daring me to challenge him.

This wasn't the night.

Jason wobbled to his feet like a new-born foal – his legs buckling and confused.

He staggered towards me, his breath so pungent, I could have set fire to it with one strike of a match.

'How was Book club? Did you have a nice evening?' he slurred, trying to look me in the eye, but his legs had a different agenda and took him back to his chair. He plonked down off centre and both Jason and the plastic chair crashed to the ground. I instinctively reached out to help him but he slapped my hand away. 'Answer my question, Lizzy: did you have a real nice evening?' He pushed the chair upright and heaved himself back to standing.

'Yes. Thank you,' I managed, tightening the belt on my mac as he stumbled towards me again. 'It was an interesting book.'

'Oh, interesting, was it?' Then louder, 'Interesting? And was your bestie there?

no talk, and we ain't having no coffee. I've got something else planned for you.'

I could feel Jason's angry heart hammering in his chest, and I glanced past him, wondering how fast I could make it down the length of the garden to the back gate – we hadn't used in years. And would the curtain of ivy, clinging to it, come away if I wrenched it open?

'Oh no you don't,' he spat, and my throat dried to a scratchy dust as I realised he'd guessed my plan. A slice of moonlight lit his knuckles as his balled fist moved towards me.

'Look!' I shouted, ducking my head, and gesturing over his shoulder to the garden behind him. The oldest trick in the book, but it worked. His grip slackened and he turned around to look.

I sprang free like a frightened child from a stranger, and ran down the garden towards the back gate with its peeling white paint and strong chains of ivy. The moon hid behind a dark cloud, plump with rain. It didn't want to watch.

I pulled at the gate and it inched open, but not enough for me to escape. I tore frantically at the vines, but Jason was soon behind me. His fingers plunged into my hair and he dragged me across the lawn towards our apple tree. My favourite tree. A tree I could sit under for hours. Just thinking. Thinking and planning. Jason pinned me against it. I turned my face away, trying to calm myself enough to think clearly by breathing in the familiar ligneous scent and focusing on the cool grain of the bark as it pressed into my cheek.

'So, I was right,' he said, with a hollow laugh. 'Why else would you run?' He squashed his fingers into my face and snapped my head around to look at him – then he took a step back. I watched his hand curl into a tight fist again, sharp knuckle bones shining through. 'You need a lesson,' he growled, a snaking vein in his temple pulsating with each word. 'Let's have this!' He made a grab for my belt and threaded it out from its loops in one fast movement. It took me by surprise, as well as the arm jerk that followed, where he flicked the belt and made a noise like a whip. Laughing, he used it to tie me to the tree with a quick, but tight knot. 'Now,' he said, his mouth contorting into a spiteful sneer, 'I'm going to chop *your* tree down and you're going to feel its pain.'

The sky darkened. The air thickened. Neither of us moved, then a drum-roll of thunder seemed to remind him of his mission. He turned and walked away.

I saw the light in Jason's tool-shed flicker on and his silhouette through the window. Could I get back to the house without him seeing me, I wondered. Break the glass door and run to Tom, waiting patiently for me in his car? I wriggled furiously, but I was as rooted to the ground as my tree was. But something hard and flat dug into me – my phone. I'd completely forgotten that I'd slid it into my back pocket earlier. I coaxed the thin fabric of my coat to the side, and squeezed my hand between the rough bark and my trembling body and managed to get hold of it.

Lightning ripped across the sky and the light in Jason's tool-shed went out.

He was coming back.

Another flash of lightening and I saw what he was carrying. The razor-sharp edge of the axe glistened as he walked steadily back down the lawn towards me.

There was a good chance I could drop my phone, but I had to try. I flicked the cover open and using my thumb scrolled through my contacts. Tania. My code name for Tom. I began to text ...*garden... quick...* I glanced up – Jason had seen the glow in my hand, realised I had my phone and had broken into a jog. I looked back down and found the arrow for send, but the phone was snatched from me. It sailed through the air and landed somewhere in a border of mixed heathers.

'Where did you get that from?' he sneered. 'Ah never mind. You won't stop this happening.'

'No!' I screamed at him. 'Please don't, Jason. Untie me. Let's go back inside. We can open a bottle of wine.'

He paused – motionless, with his axe raised above his head. 'You know what, that's not a bad idea.'

My knees buckled and I slumped against the tree. *Thank God*.

'Yeah, a drink's a great idea. I'll fetch myself another beer.' He dropped the axe and stepped into my space. With his lips close enough to kiss me, he added, 'a bit of sustenance to help me swing my axe into this tree of yours is a real good idea.' He walked away.

I tried to slide myself downwards, maybe escape by getting under my belt, but got no further than my chest. I threw a longing look at the back gate – I had to get out of here, then I heard Jason coming back. He was laughing.

He'd tied the knot around the back of the tree, so I tried to twist it around but it was snagging on something and stuck fast.

'Cheers,' Jason called, arriving back in front of me, and raising his bottle in the air. Every smell on him seemed to have doubled in strength, and I thought I might be sick. He picked up the axe again and began to circle the tree. My neck prickled when he disappeared from sight, but he was soon back in front of me. 'This might take a while,' he grinned. 'Keep yer fingers in.'

I closed my eyes, but they sprang open when I heard the splintering. The sound of wood breaking, but not my tree – a door. The gate! Pieces of white-painted wood littered the grass. First Tom's arm appeared as he punched through the gate, then his foot. He was here.

Jason's jaw dropped as he watched Tom break through the back gate into our garden, but then Jason's posture shifted from shock to fearless, and he planted his feet wide and firm.

Tom stepped clumsily over the debris, then froze as he took in the scene. Within seconds he was speeding towards us. I glanced back at Jason, a smirk on his face, and with both hands holding the axe, his fingers were working into a better grip.

Tom! No!

I brought my knee up, and luckily with Jason still close enough to reach, I thrust my knee into his groin. Hard. And as I executed that one swift movement it felt as if my tree had seeped all of its power into me.

Jason howled, his drunken eyes bulging, before crumpling over and folding himself into a ball at my feet.

I heard Tom behind the tree fumbling with the knot, and my belt fell loose. I collapsed into his arms, clinging to him as if he were a floating life jacket amidst a shipwreck.

'Everything will be alright,' Tom promised, as we walked around Jason, still writhing in pain on the damp grass.

'My car's just out here. Hurry,' Tom urged, as we clambered over the debris from the broken gate.

I suddenly had a thought. Slipping my hand from his, I turned back towards the garden.

'Lizzy?' Tom called after me. 'What are you doing? Don't go back!'

But I had one last thing to do.

Jason was still on the ground, the axe within inches of his fingertips - I saw his eyes dart, but I pounced on the axe before he could. And ran.

'Open the boot!' I shouted to Tom, as I staggered back through the gate with it. 'We're taking this.'

"Why?' Tom asked grabbing the axe from me.

'My tree,' I panted, '*it* helped me. I had to save *it*.'

THE SILK SCARF

E ve sat at her dressing table and held her hand out before her to admire her wedding ring.

If she closed her eyes, she could almost feel Albie placing it onto her finger three wonderful years ago. Dear Albie. Already – she missed him so much.

The sound of distant hooves on gravel disturbed her memories. Eve went to the window and peered down at the driveway below. Her blue-grey eyes, although tired with age, were still sharp and she sought out her stable boy, who, as every morning, would be leading her cherished white mare, Angel, towards the house.

Eve smiled. Yes, there they were.

Phillip looked up at Eve's window and she waved – her signal to him that she was on her way. But his usual response, a salute in return, never came. Instead, Phillip turned away. Distracted maybe, Eve considered, or perhaps keen for her to hurry down and take Angel for her daily canter and allow him to get on with other tasks. Phillip certainly was one of their most hardworking members of staff.

Returning to her dressing table, Eve hastily pulled a brush through her hair, but as she did, the previous day's events came flooding back like a sudden ice-cold shower...

Eve remembered walking along the church path behind the six men carrying the satin-smooth mahogany coffin. An impressive shower of white lilies covered the casket, their fragrance filling the air she stepped through. The name engraved on the brass plate underneath them all – Albert James Winston. Eve's beloved Albi.

The congregation were mainly all seated inside, but Eve, her family, and the vicar came in last. There was a shuffle of feet as the small group entered the vestibule, shoulders hunched in thick black coats brushing up against each other and polite murmurs as to who should go ahead.

Amanda, her sweet face streaked with tears for her father, moved to Eve's side, and they made their way down the aisle, their footsteps in unison, along with everyone's likely perception of their relationship. Eve's eyes remained focused on the box gliding slowly through the church in front of them. She would have gladly taken her stepdaughter's arm but knew it would be fruitless to try. And besides, Amanda now clung to Fergus, her own husband, who was very much alive, and had quickly taken his position to Amanda's right.

It wasn't until the funeral was over, and the last mourners had left Tarnstone Manor that Amanda's husband finally revealed his true feelings towards his wife's stepmother.

His harsh words swelling Eve's grief until her heart felt as if it may crumble under the pressure.

'That pink scarf you wore was completely inappropriate,' Fergus had jeered as Eve followed them into the warm kitchen. Eve had dismissed the kitchen staff, after they had served an exquisite array of food, they'd prepared for Albi's wake, insisting they took a few hours off now to be with their own grief.

But Amanda had wanted some more tea to calm her nerves and Fergus had offered to make it. 'I have no idea what you were thinking,' he continued to address Eve's rebellious action of adding a touch of colour to the traditional all-black attire expected at a funeral. He strode into the scullery, snatching the kettle from the stove and filling it with such speed, the water had sprayed all over the window.

'Mrs Colby won't be happy with you,' Amanda had joked. Eve knew that although Amanda had very little time for her, she was at least, in this moment, trying to lighten the mood.

'Well, Mrs Colby...' Fergus dumped the kettle down and lit the stove, '... won't be here for much longer.'

'She's handed her notice in?' Eve asked, scraping her chair back and standing in shock not to have heard.

'No, she hasn't,' Amanda said fast, 'but Fergus wants to make a few changes now that...' she slid a long grip from her hat as if it had been piercing her skull, '...now Daddy's gone, and well, Mrs Colby's on Fergus's list. That's all.'

'Who else is on your list Fergus?' Eve narrowed her eyes at her step son-in-law.

He held her gaze. 'You still haven't explained the hideous pink scarf, Eve.' His thin eyebrows shifted upwards as he took the seat opposite her.

'Albie bought it for me on our honeymoon,' Eve had recalled in a whisper. 'He knew I loved raspberries and it's the exact colour of the variety we have in our garden.' Eve fingered the soft silky fabric. 'He loved me to wear it.'

Eve placed her brush back down and shivered – it was exceptionally cold today, she thought, rubbing her arms with icy fingers. She glanced outside – no sign of a breeze, and the sky was a soft cornflower blue. It felt calm – she felt calm. And peaceful.

Eve dabbed a little perfume on her wrist, and stood up to leave, but her hand moved to her throat as another memory floated towards her. Fergus. She recalled him barging into her bedroom last night. His mission to deliver more opinions – his sharp words coming for her as rapid as gun fire. She had told him that she would not be bullied from her home, that he was wasting his breath. But he would not listen.

Eve's fingers caressed her neck, as she remembered Fergus tearing her beautiful pink scarf from her; her delicate skin still smarting from where the silk had swiftly uncurled, then tightened again around her throat.

Eve pushed the memory aside and picked up her riding crop to leave. If this small family were to all remain under the same roof, as Albie would have wished, then bridges would need to be repaired. But now the fresh air, and the thought of Angel's welcoming nudge, beckoned.

But as Eve walked towards the bedroom door she stopped. Her crop slipping from her fingers as she suddenly saw a woman lying still and pale on the bed – her blue-grey eyes wide open and... empty.

Eve moved closer.

Wasn't that *her* own arm draped lifelessly over the side of the bed? Of course, it was, because there, wound tightly around her neck was the beautiful silk scarf Albie had always loved her to wear.

SMELLY CHEESE

C onnie has just taken off for the evening. A blur of orange fake-fur and tassel-fringed boots. She's gone to one of her book-club thingy nights.

And with only moments after slamming the front door behind her – always a slam, never a click – she's back.

'My books!' She grabs her forgotten bag slumped on the bottom stair. It's so full of books, notepads and writing-related junk, that it looks more like Santa's sack than a handbag. 'That's you distracting me again,' Connie says. 'Oh, and I got cash out,' she informs me with a triumphant final slam.

I asked a woman at the bank once if they had some kind of razor-sharp screen that could slide down when it detected my wife's pin-number. *Her number, my money.* And preferably, I'd added, capable of simultaneously slicing off her fingers. The woman thought I was joking.

'Of course, you did,' I mutter to myself, as I hear Connie's new car purr from our drive and into the night. It's impossible for my wife to leave the house without a wad of tenner's in her purse.

It's been three years since she gave up that nice little earner over at the Legion, and now it's muggins here that must put the extra graft in to keep her fridge full and her wardrobe stocked.

Twenty-five years I've worked at Brindle's Gas Works. That place is no good for my condition, but Connie just shrugs when I bring it up.

'Have some patience, Pete,' she always says. 'I'll get a book deal soon. Six figures no doubt.'

So, here I am – her out and me in, with a little time for myself. I pick up the remote and flick through the channels; nothing decent on. No footie at any rate. I turn it off. Perhaps I'll tackle the crossword. I hunt for a pencil and find one of hers – pink, with the words *Let Your Imagination Soar* stamped on it.

I give my neck a stretch and crack my knuckles. I've had an idea. Why don't I try my hand at this writing game? How hard can it be to write one book?

I mean how many more hot, sweaty, gas-fume-filled hours will I have to endure at Brindle's, before Connie actually sells something she's written? I toss my newspaper aside and reach for one of her notebooks instead. There are plenty to choose from: stripy to spotty, frog covered, or gold bleeding plated. Her flippin notebooks are everywhere.

She even sleeps with one under her pillow – can you believe it? And then there's this proper annoying habit she has whenever I ask her what she's writing about. She taps the end of her nose three times, real slow-like and says, 'Now, Pete, that would be telling – wouldn't it?'

I settle back onto the sofa, imagining how her eyes will pop when I tell her I've had a call from a publisher before she has. It will be bye bye Gas Works, hello retirement, good health and a peaceful life. Although I shouldn't get carried away, *she'll* still be in it.

I stare at a blank page. Clear my throat. Stare some more. I put the notepad down and fetch a beer.

Back on the sofa, and I swing my feet up and stretch my legs out. The soles of my slippers push against one of Connie's precious red and black velvet cushions. They're rock hard. She probably had them stuffed with notebooks.

'What's the point in these?' I asked her when they'd first appeared. 'There's no give in them.'

'I could say the same about you,' she'd quipped, on route to answering the front door. Our weekly take-away had just arrived.

I try squashing one with my foot. Squeeze the hell out of it, and almost break my toe.

I stare at the blank page again. Perhaps hunger is causing my writer's block. I consider fetching a couple of mini pork pies and a packet of crisps without a plate. I think better of it. Connie can spot a crumb like an ant at a picnic.

The room feels chilly, which is probably why my fingers aren't working properly.

Our electric fire with its fake logs is unplugged. Course it is. Connie has a habit of turning things off when she goes out, as if she were leaving the house for a week's holiday. Oblivious, it seems, that I'm still in it. And as usual, she has switched off the central heating on her way out tonight.

'You'll be alright, Pete,' she told me. 'Only slim men feel the cold.'

I need a title for my book. That'll be as good a place to start as any. The Igloo?

The Dying Man? Mmm... I look around our living room for inspiration and spot one of Connie's *How To Write* books under the TV. I roll off the sofa and swipe it up.

Chapter One: *Write what you know.*

Alright I know a lot of stuff, but *trying to avoid the hazards of working with molten metal* probably won't make the next Bestsellers list. I look around the room again and see my watercolour of Desert Orchid tucked away on a narrow bit of wall near the curtains. The only wall-space Connie will allow me. I painted it a long time ago. I would have loved to paint more, but apparently whilst we live in such a small house, there's only room for one of us to indulge in a creative hobby. Ah, but Dessie. What a magnificent stallion though: pale grey to begin with, becoming white with age. Not unlike myself. It triggers a memory. I remember a really cracking day out I had last summer with my two best mates: Stinky Jack and George Finch, affectionally known as Tiny. We hit the races, had a few beers, and made a few bets. Tiny, a professional jockey in his youth, picks out the winners as regular as Connie picks out all the good biscuits from our tin.

'The Lady Constance!' Tiny had insisted, as we all studied the form for the last race. '*And* it's a horse named after your wife, Pete. It's a no-brainer.'

The Lady Constance won. Easily. Then straight after the race her owner put her up for sale. Me and the lads had a chuckle over our chances of buying her between us.

Stinky Jack has a fish stall down the market and still lives with his mum, so he has a fair few bob stashed away. Tiny lost his wife a couple of years back – lucky sod – and we reckoned he wasn't short of a few quid either. But I got a wife whose favourite four words are: *I got cash out*. So that was it. We didn't buy The Lady Constance. But perhaps, I think, blowing heat into my fingers, there's a story in there somewhere.

I scratch my chin, fetch another beer, and turn the page.

Chapter Two: *What if*

Start with a *What if* the author advises. I can do that. I get up and turn the fire on.

What if we'd bought that lovely little filly that day? Where would I have got my share of the money from? I push against the brick-hard cushions and they both fall off the sofa. Thud, thud. On the floor. As the fire begins to warm the room, an idea sparks. *What if* the other Constance – my ball and chain, had an accident? A tragic and fatal accident.

I sit up, pencil ready.

What if the insurance pay-out had been exactly the right amount to buy my share of *Lady Constance* the wonder horse? Oh yes. I congratulate myself for the sheer genius of it. I decide to switch on the fake-log-effect on the fire to celebrate. A red glow fills the room. Nice and cosy. I bet she's wrong, I think, rubbing my hands together, as a very unpleasant burning-dust smell fills the room, about the amount of electricity this uses.

Chapter Three. *Plot*

I read on. Another beer and I have plots coming out of my ears. In fact, it's my beer that leads me to a real juicy one. Frank, the landlord down at the Nag's Head, shared with me once how he managed to keep rats out of his cellar.

'I hide poison inside bits of cheese. Stupid rodents,' he had laughed, 'you'd think that'd be obvious.'

So now, what would happen if a little rat poison ended up in Connie's belly? She loves her cheese. Eats it with everything. No. I stand corrected. She just eats everything.

Ha ha... move over Alfred Hitchcock. Pete has arrived.

I race onto Chapter Four: *Motive*.

Right, this is easy. Connie gave Frank the brush off once. Or so she said. She'd been doing a couple of evenings a week behind the bar for him at the time.

Apparently, he touched her bum, and she gave him a right dressing down in front of his punters, *and* threatened to tell his wife. If it were true, that would give Frank a tidy little reason to polish her off. Motive sorted. And there was me thinking I would have to be the murderer.

I set myself up in the kitchen to make a list of the most suitable cheeses to use.

The hard ones, like Mature Cheddar, could crack when you inserted the poison. Feta maybe? Although that might crumble. Something softer like Brie could work, or a good strong-tasting Blue, which would also be useful for disguising the taste of the poison.

The Mrs *loves* stilton.

I'm just checking to see if rat poison has a colour when I hear the slam of Connie's car door. She's home. I close the fridge and the cupboard door under the sink.

I rush into the hall to see her large silhouette hovering outside the front door. As her key scratches around for the lock, I dodge back into the living room to switch the fire off and shove the notebook under the sofa. No. She'll find it. I grab one of her lead cushions and unzip it.

'Hi,' I call, hearing her shuffle up the hallway. I have a few seconds to spare because she's heading in her usual direction – the kitchen.

I come up behind her as she shoves her size eights into purple fluffy slippers.

'They have no taste,' Connie complains. But I have no idea who *they* are because she likes to keep the identities of her friends a secret. 'Who plans a Writers' Retreat in England?' she continues, sliding a dinner plate from the cupboard and dumping it on the work surface with a clunk. 'Everyone knows the French Riviera is far more inspiring.'

And there's me thinking she doesn't like the heat. I pull out a chair and sit down.

Connie's eyes narrow. 'Why is it so warm in here, Pete?'

'Search me.' I shrug, as she reaches past me to tug open the fridge door. The pungent odour of Roquefort and Gorgonzola hit me in the face like a snog from a skunk. I watch her stare at the contents for a moment before making her selection. I notice there's enough space on the middle shelf to fit her head – if she's keen enough to cool down.

With her plate of cheeses, two cold chicken legs and a scotch egg in one hand, and a carton of cookie-dough flavoured milk in the other, Connie shoves the fridge door shut with her elbow. 'I'm off to bed,' she tells me, shuffling towards the hall.

'Enjoy your supper,' I say, an image having just dropped into my head from the grotty staff kitchen at Brindle's, of the boss sprinkling a little rat poison in a damp corner – and it was blue.

Connie squints at me through her extra set of lashes, then reverses back into the kitchen.

'What are you smiling about, Pete?' She sits down opposite me with the delicacy of an elephant in a deckchair. 'What have *you* been plotting this evening, Pete?' she asks, before sinking her teeth into a large chunk of smoked gruyere.

I tap the end of my nose three times, real slow like. 'Now, Connie,' I say, 'that would be telling – wouldn't it?'